"Don't get dressed on my account."

Kelsey looked up.

No clean shirt, no baby. Just one hundred percent, mouth-watering—cowboy.

"Cooper."

He crossed the room in a heartbeat, swore softly under his breath before his mouth captured hers in a searing kiss.

Kelsey wound her hands around his neck, meeting his kiss head-on, pressing her curves to the hard planes of his chest. His hands brushed her sweat jacket from her shoulders. He broke free of her mouth, his lips moving along her jaw until he nipped at her ear.

"I wasn't going to do this," he whispered hotly, "but you said my name..."

Dear Reader,

As a fan of the many sagas of the Fortune family over the years, I was thrilled when, as a relatively new author, I was asked to be part of the Lost...and Found continuity. When I read the outline for my book, my first thought was "Oh, a baby changes everything" and little Anthony certainly does that for Cooper Fortune.

There's a saying that goes something like, "Becoming a parent is a decision to forever have your heart go walking around outside your body." Something this wandering cowboy—who suddenly finds himself a father—never experienced before his son came into his life. Add a chance meeting with a pretty horse trainer and Cooper's world is about to be changed in ways he never dreamed of.

It was such fun to be with Cooper and Kelsey as they found their way to each other and their happily ever after. I hope you enjoy their journey!

Happy reading!

Christyne

FORTUNE'S SECRET BABY

CHRISTYNE BUTLER

Harlequin®

SPECIAL EDITION

Special thanks and acknowledgment to
Christyne Butler for her contribution to
The Fortunes of Texas: Lost…and Found.

Recycling programs
for this product may
not exist in your area.

ISBN-13: 978-0-373-65596-0

FORTUNE'S SECRET BABY

Copyright © 2011 by Harlequin Books S.A.

Books by Christyne Butler

Special Edition

The Cowboy's Second Chance #1980
The Sheriff's Secret Wife #2022
*A Daddy for Jacoby #2089
†Fortune's Secret Baby #2114

*Welcome to Destiny
† The Fortunes of Texas: Lost…and Found

CHRISTYNE BUTLER

fell in love with romance novels while serving in the United States Navy and started writing her own stories six years ago. She considers selling to Special Edition a dream come true and enjoys writing contemporary romances full of life, love, a hint of laughter and perhaps a dash of danger, too. And there has to be a happily-ever-after or she's just not satisfied.

She lives with her family in central Massachusetts and loves to hear from her readers at chris@christynebutler.com. Or visit her website at www.christynebutler.com.

To the terrific writers I worked with on this continuity:
Allison Leigh, Judy Duarte, Susan Crosby,
Marie Ferrarella and Victoria Pade,
and Susan Litman...
the editor who brought us all together!

Chapter One

Thirteen steps.

The length of the baby's room, from the crib near the bay window to the doorway at the opposite corner, could be covered in thirteen steps.

Cooper Fortune had been counting, repeatedly, for the last interminably long twenty minutes while the squirming five-month-old in his arms wailed loud enough to wake the dead.

Anthony, middle name still unknown, Fortune. His son. A child he'd only known existed for the last week and a half.

Probability of paternity = 99.99%.

That's what the laboratory had told him when they'd called with the results and in the blink of an eye, Cooper Fortune—wandering cowboy—had a child.

"Looks like you lost the parent lottery." Cooper spoke above the baby's cries as he paced the small room, cradling the flailing infant against his chest. "Welcome to the club, buddy. My folks were lousy, too."

He had no memory of his father, and Cooper's mother, Cindy Fortune, a former showgirl and wannabe socialite, easily held the number-one spot on the list of worst mothers in the history of the world.

"Of course, we still don't know what happened to *your* mama," Cooper continued, noticing the decibel level of the baby's cries, not to mention the wiggle factor, had lessened as soon as he started talking. "But your Uncle Ross is on the case and I'm sure he'll find her soon. I wish I knew why she left you and how the hel—heck you ended up here in Red Rock."

And why Lulu never bothered to tell him she was pregnant.

He'd met Lulu Carlton at a local bar about a year and a half ago while working on a ranch in Rock Country, Minnesota. They dated for about six months, but when Cooper's job ended, so had the relationship. Anthony's estimated birth date was around the middle of December, which meant the child was conceived just before Cooper hightailed it out of Minnesota early last year.

And didn't that make him feel like a loser?

As he stared down at the little bundle looking up at him with a curious gaze from familiar dark brown eyes, Cooper had no idea what to do next.

"This isn't working out too well, huh, partner? We haven't exactly had much one-on-one time, until tonight. And usually you're a bit quieter."

Cooper watched the baby rub at his eyes with tiny fists. The crying lowered to a soft whimpering for a moment. Could the pacing and talking actually be working?

He slowly headed for the crib. Maybe he could get back downstairs before the end of the Red Sox/Rangers game he'd been watching in between reading a book that promised to tell him everything he needed to know about dealing with a baby. He leaned over the railing, making sure to support Anthony's head like he'd seen Kirsten do numerous times, but the moment the kid went horizontal, the screams returned.

"Okay, so you're not ready to concede." Cooper gathered the baby to his chest and started walking again, patting Anthony gently on his back. "Boy, you got some lungs on you. I don't recollect you putting up this much of a fuss before."

Cooper had slept in the spare bedroom downstairs for three nights before he'd heard a peep out of the kid after bedtime. At first he hadn't known what the noise was. Heck, it sounded a bit like a baby calf bellowing for its mama.

"But by the time I hightailed it up here, Miss Kirsten already had things taken care of, huh? Not tonight, though. Tonight, it's just you and me—"

"What's going on? Is he okay?"

He turned toward the feminine voice. His cousin's fiancée, Kirsten Allen, stood at the doorway. When Anthony let loose another howl, she crossed the room in a heartbeat and reached for the baby.

And Cooper let her take him.

His first instinct had been to keep hold of his son, but Anthony had stuck out his little arms for the petite brunette as soon as he saw her.

"Oh, sweetie, what's all this crying about?" Kirsten cooed as she held the child close. "It's okay now, I've got you."

Cooper crossed his arms over his chest, ignoring the pang in his heart at her words.

"He's been bawling like that for close to a half hour now," he said when she looked at him. "He calmed down some, but I guess that was just a rest before he revved up again."

"Is he wet? Did you check his diaper?"

Diaper?

Damn! Cooper let his silence answer her.

Kirsten walked to the changing table and laid Anthony down on the padded cushion. "What about a bottle?" she asked, her tone softer, matching Anthony's now-quiet fussing while making quick work of changing the baby. "It's been a few hours since he last ate. Did you make up a bottle for him from the formula we left on the kitchen counter?"

Strike two. The thought of a bottle never crossed his mind. "I'll go get one now."

She paused in closing up a fresh diaper on the baby to look at him. "Cooper, I'm sorry. I don't mean to sound so—"

"Don't worry about it." He waved off her apology and headed for the doorway. "Be back in a minute."

Seconds later, he walked into the kitchen but stopped at the sight of his cousin, Jeremy Fortune, a can of powdered formula and jug of filtered water in front of him, mixing up a bottle.

Cooper leaned against the door frame and fought not to react to the unnamed emotion bubbling up inside him at the sight of the doctor who looked so at ease fixing a meal for *his* son.

But life in general was easy for his cousin; being one of the *good* Fortunes made it so for him and his four brothers, all of whom had found success, both professionally and in their personal lives. Cooper and his siblings had never had it easy despite sharing the Fortune name, a name that carried a lot of respect and admiration, not only in Red Rock, but all of Texas.

Then again, Cooper's brother, Ross, and their sister, Frannie, both had finally found happiness and love over the last year and his other brother, Flint, had made a name for himself as a fine arts dealer.

So where did that leave him?

Up until a couple of weeks ago, he'd lived a good life with a few simple guidelines: Always do the best job you can. A healthy bank account was more important than material belongings. Avoid stepping on another man's toes where the ladies were concerned.

And no putting down roots. Better to be a rolling stone than a moss-covered rock stuck in one place. That last one led easily to the most important rule of all.

Never marry or have kids.

No sense getting involved when his personal history made it clear he was never going to be any good at it. Being a wandering cowboy, moving from ranch to ranch, job to job, came as natural to him as breathing.

Happily ever after? Not for him.

Scrubbing his face with his hand, Cooper pulled his mind from the past to deal with the here and now. He wasn't angry, at least not with Jeremy or Kirsten. They were only doing what they knew was right for Anthony.

Was he pissed at himself for not remembering the basics Kirsten had tried to drill into his head for the last ten days? Or was it something more—a sense of defeat, of loss?

When Anthony had pulled away from him and reached for the woman who'd been taking care of him for the last four months, he felt like he'd been kicked in the gut by a wayward horse hoof.

"Ah, I guess I beat you to bottle duty." Jeremy finally noticed Cooper standing there. "We heard Anthony crying when we walked in. I told Kirsten to let you handle things, but she lasted less than five minutes before heading upstairs. I figured having a second bottle ready to go wouldn't hurt."

Cooper smiled, hoping for the practiced grin he'd refined back in high school that had charmed everyone from cheerleaders to the local sheriff deputies. "You figured right."

Jeremy secured a clear plastic cap over the nipple and tossed the bottle in Cooper's direction.

He grabbed it midair. "Why don't you take it upstairs?" Cooper asked. "I figured I'd catch the end of the game."

His cousin just shook his head. "He's your kid, Daddy."

That was the first time someone had called him that and it hit Cooper right between the eyes. Hell, he hadn't said the word to himself yet.

"What?" Jeremy asked.

Cooper shook his head. "Nothing."

"Look, I know this…this whole situation is the craziest thing we've ever had to deal with—"

"With this family?"

A slight frown slipped over Jeremy's face. "Okay, the craziest thing *you've* had to deal with since you headed out for greener pastures twenty-odd years ago, but you're doing... You seem to be working hard at figuring everything out."

"Yeah."

His cousin put the jug of water into the refrigerator before turning back. "You know, finding out she wasn't Anthony's aunt was a bit of a shock for Kirsten. She and her brother believed the baby was his after his ex-girlfriend left Anthony with them."

Cooper had already heard this crazy story.

When they'd managed to finally find the ex-girlfriend, she admitted neither she nor Kirsten's brother were the baby's true parents and that another man she was involved with gave her the baby to care for. Then the ex-girlfriend skipped town. The police were still trying to find her.

"If that gold medallion hadn't been left with Anthony," Jeremy continued, "who knows if we would've ever connected the baby to your side of the family."

Cooper nodded. The medallion was one of four identical coins given to him and his siblings years ago as a Christmas gift from their mother. He hadn't even realized it was missing from the inside zippered pocket of his duffle bag all these months.

"It's been hard for Kirsten, but she's happy you two have found your way to each other. She just wants what's best for everyone. What's best for Anthony."

And you aren't it.

The words weren't spoken, but Cooper got the message.

Loud and clear.

"Are you nuts?" Flint Fortune took a long swallow before returning his beer bottle to the table with a loud thud. "Moving out? Living alone with Anthony? You've been in the kid's life two weeks!"

Cooper ignored his younger brother and concentrated on Ross, the older one, who sat across from him in a booth at Red, a celebrated family restaurant in Red Rock. Owned by José and Maria Mendoza, Red was managed by one of their many offspring, Marcos, who'd sat the Fortune brothers in a corner booth to allow for private conversation.

Ross eyed him over the rim of his own beer, one brow raised.

"I've been thinking about this for a few days." Cooper answered Ross's unspoken question, his thumb tracing patterns in the condensation on his glass of iced tea. "I know it's the right thing for me. And for Anthony."

Taking a mouthful of tea to soothe his parched throat, Cooper reminded himself again why he'd sworn off alcohol the night he'd found out about his son.

There was no way his child would ever associate the stale odor of booze with a parental touch. The few times Cindy had displayed halfhearted affection to Cooper, the embrace always reeked of perfume, cigarette smoke and whatever drink she'd chosen as her favorite cocktail of that week.

"You've had a rough couple of weeks. First Anthony, and then finding out Lulu had been dead all these months instead of just a runaway parent. You sure this isn't misplaced guilt?" Ross finally asked.

"No."

"Identifying a former girlfriend's remains in a morgue is something I never want on my 'to-do' list," Ross continued. "And giving her a proper burial yesterday was a decent thing to do."

"Lulu didn't have any family. I did what needed to be done. I still wish I knew why she never tried to find me."

"Well, we guessed she came to Red Rock back in January to see you because she'd read the news about William and Lily's wedding." Flint shoved a forkful of fajitas and guacamole into his mouth and quickly chewed. "The forensics report did say her car accident happened around that date."

"That still doesn't explain how my son ended up with Kirsten's brother's ex-girlfriend. Unless Lulu purposely left the baby with her," Cooper said.

"Or why Lulu didn't try to contact you long before the baby was born," Ross added.

"Not that you would've been easy to find," Flint said. "Hell, you finally got your first cell phone a week ago. Welcome to the twenty-first century, bro."

The device was a necessity now because of the baby, and Cooper still wasn't used to the contraption clipped to his belt. Still, even if he'd had a cell phone last year, would he have shared the number with Lulu?

"Lulu wasn't happy I was leaving town, but it's not like she begged me to stick around." Cooper pushed at the food on his plate, his appetite suddenly gone. "We both made it clear from the beginning neither of us was interested in settling down. You guys know me, my life is—was—about being a cowboy, being free to go where I want, when I want. Maybe Lulu figured it was best if I wasn't in the kid's life at all."

"But now you are."

He let the fork drop to the plate. "Yes, and I need one-on-one time with my son if we're ever going to find our way."

"You don't plan on leaving town, do you?" Ross asked.

Cooper shook his head. "No. Red Rock is home. The Fortunes are here and they're Anthony's family."

"Damn right we are."

All three brothers looked up to find JR Fortune standing at the table. The oldest of their Uncle William's five sons, JR had left a successful life in Los Angeles last year to put down roots in Red Rock. He'd purchased a local ranch, renamed it after his deceased mother and went to work restoring the land and the buildings.

"JR." Cooper greeted his cousin as he sat next to him.

"Things a bit crowded at my brother's place?" JR asked.

Cooper nodded and quickly told the men at the table what happened two weeks ago and how he hadn't had a moment alone with his son since. "I know I didn't come up with the diaper or bottle answer right away that night, but I would've. I just never got the chance to think that far ahead."

"Well, I have an idea that might work," JR said. "Your stallion's been staying at my place since you got back into town. We've got room for you and the baby, too."

Cooper shook his head. The main house at his cousin's ranch, Molly's Pride, came with three times the square footage of Jeremy and Kirsten's, but that wasn't what he was looking for. "I appreciate you taking in Solo when I got to town and keeping an eye on him, but—"

"I'm not talking about staying in the hacienda with me and Isabella. There are a couple of furnished cottages on the place sitting empty. You and Anthony are welcome to one of them. It would give you two the independence it sounds like you're looking for, but with family nearby…just in case."

Glancing at his brothers, Cooper watched them nod in agreement. It was a good idea. He missed being on a ranch and he missed Solo, the buckskin stallion he'd picked up outside Laramie, Wyoming, six years ago and named after his favorite movie character. The horse had quickly become his best friend.

"Okay, but only if the place is far away from your house. Anthony's got quite a set of lungs on him and he's not afraid to use them."

JR chuckled then said, "That's fine with me, but we need to get used to the idea of baby noises around the ranch. Isabella is already decorating the nursery for our bambino."

They sealed the agreement with a handshake and another round of beers for everyone—except Cooper, who asked for a refill on his sweetened iced tea.

As the setting sun cast a blaze of deep reds, bright oranges and soft pinks across the Texas sky, Cooper felt pretty damn proud of himself. He and Anthony were all moved into a two-bedroom stucco cottage. Ross, Jeremy and JR had helped with moving the baby furniture that Jeremy and Kirsten had insisted Cooper take with him.

Telling them about his decision had been hard, but they'd agreed it was the best idea for everyone, even as Kirsten flagged pages in his *Parenting for Dummies* book and programmed their phone numbers into his cell phone.

JR's wife, Isabella, who ran her own interior design business from the ranch, had decorated the cottage with sturdy furniture and accents of bright Southwest colors. The miniature hacienda came complete with a swing on the covered front porch, a fully stocked kitchen and bedding for the queen-size bed in the bigger of the two bedrooms. With the smaller bedroom filled with everything Anthony needed, Cooper had to admit it felt good to be on his own again.

On his own plus one.

"Time for bed, little guy," Cooper whispered, rising from the rocking chair, the bottle releasing from the baby's mouth with a gentle pop.

It'd taken three tries to get the consistency of the bedtime bottle right, but he considered that a victory after they'd sampled a half dozen different jars of baby food before finding a flavor Anthony would eat without sending it flying through the air in disgust.

Making his way to the crib, Cooper stepped over the remains of a handful of disposable diapers on the floor. Who knew the sticky tabs on those suckers ripped off so easily? But his son was on his way to dreamland, that's all that mattered.

Laying the boy on his back, Cooper paused for a moment, awed by the tightening in his chest as he looked at his son. Unable to stop himself, he lightly touched the unbelievable softness of one chubby cheek. Anthony's fists waved in the air and Cooper backed away. Turning on the baby monitor on the nearby dresser, he grabbed the smaller handheld version and left the darkened room.

Drawn to the kitchen by the smell of freshly brewed coffee he'd made himself earlier but never got to taste, he poured a mug and paused to listen to the silence.

He wasn't used to this.

Usually he spent his evenings at a local honky-tonk, in the company of fellow cowboys with a beer in one hand and a fistful of cards in the other, or on occasion, it was just him and his horse.

Ignoring the itch to visit his friend tucked away in the main barn, Cooper turned away from the mess in the kitchen and walked into the living room. He placed the baby monitor on the coffee table and reached for the parenting book he'd been reading for the last couple of weeks. The image of a smiling family graced the cover.

Had his father and mother ever looked at each other that way? At him? He doubted it. His father had taken off for greener pastures before Cooper had turned two, and Cindy was an indifferent parent at best.

What kind of parent had Lulu been? How had she dealt with being alone and pregnant? And what had finally driven her all this way to find him? Hadn't she wanted the baby anymore?

Sighing, he settled back in his chair and cracked open the book, his mind focused on Anthony. Less than six months old and the kid was already the ultimate story of luck gone bad—a motherless child who was now stuck with *him* for a dad.

A little while later, cries jerked Cooper out of the arms of an unknown woman in a strange but enticing dream. Stumbling out of the chair and tripping over his boots lying nearby, he raced down the short hallway to the baby's room.

He rubbed the sleep from his eyes and found Anthony still on his back, the angelic look gone from his face and replaced with eyes clenched tightly together and his tiny mouth letting loose an ear-piercing screech.

"Hey, buddy, what's going on?" He reached for the baby, who continued his crying. "Geesh, you're not a happy camper."

First stop, the changing table. Cooper made quick work of the baby's diaper, thankful it was only wet and not one of the industrial-strength, poop-filled ones Anthony favored at times.

He peered at the clock and saw that it was just short of midnight. "Okay, so you must be ready for another fill-up. Good thing I've got another bottle cooling in the fridge, but you can tone it down any time now."

Anthony either didn't care or thought his daddy wasn't moving fast enough, because the crying only increased as Cooper headed for the kitchen. His tone doubled when he saw the bottle.

"Hold on, partner. You don't want cold cow juice." Cooper juggled the baby with one arm while popping the bottle into the electric warmer. "Hang on just another five minutes."

Anthony was hanging on, but not quietly. He fussed and squirmed while Cooper counted down the minutes on the warmer. Finally done, he shook the bottle and it took some maneuvering to test its contents to make sure it wasn't too hot. Then he popped the bottle into Anthony's waiting mouth.

The peace and quiet only lasted a few seconds.

"Easy there, you're going to drown yourself." Cooper pulled the bottle back as Anthony continued to cry, spitting up more of the liquid than he was taking in. "Okay, you don't want the milk. What do you want?"

Anthony's only answer was increased wailing.

He held the baby close to his chest and walked. Around the dining table, into the living room, down the hall and back again. He didn't bother to count his steps this time as he gently patted Anthony on the back. Thankful for the dim glow from the night-light in the baby's room and the light over the stove, he made it through the furniture obstacle course without stubbing his toe or bashing an ankle.

Now if he could only get the little guy to calm down.

"You liked it when I talked to you last time we were in this situation." Keeping his voice low, Cooper never stopped moving or talking. "Maybe that'll work again? But what the heck do I say to someone whose only response is an attempt to break my eardrums?"

Three hours later…three million steps.

Okay, maybe not three million, but it had to be close.

Cooper figured he'd shared his entire life story with the kid, starting with stories of growing up with Ross, Flint and Frannie—the four of them against the world— as they struggled to keep things going despite living with their wayward mother.

He told him about the time he and Ross taught Frannie how to ride a bicycle without training wheels, and when he'd taken on a bully twice his size after the kid refused to stop messing with Flint. Stories of high school, his rodeo days and taking college classes at a variety of places around the country until he finally earned his degree in animal husbandry. He even included every joke he could remember that might be appropriate for little ears.

He'd only paused long enough to grab a few sips of tepid tap water, not wanting to get a mug of hot coffee anywhere near the baby. Man, what he wouldn't give for a cup of joe....

Anthony had moments of lesser crying, but he never really stopped and Cooper was getting worried. He reached for his cell phone and flipped it open. Pressing the "contacts" button, he saw Jeremy and Kirsten's number listed first.

But he couldn't make the call. He and Anthony needed to make it through together. On their own.

The baby wasn't warm so he figured he wasn't running a fever. He was just cranky and probably missing the familiar surroundings of his former home, but Cooper had never been the one to comfort him. Someone else was always there to take Anthony off his hands. Now, he was the only person his son could rely on, and he was determined to make it work.

"You're aiming to break the crying record, aren't ya?" Cooper whispered. "I don't know where you get your energy."

Another diaper change, more tries with the bottle, making use of the rocking chair next to the crib.

Nothing worked.

"How about some music? What's that saying about music soothing the savage beast?" He looked around for a radio, but there were none in the cottage. "Well, I hope you like country, because I don't know any baby songs."

He started with the classics from Johnny Cash and worked his way up to Garth Brooks, making up words when the real ones wouldn't come. He tried the bottle again during his rendition of "Friends in Low Places" and the baby latched on to it. When it was empty, Anthony kept fussing, so Cooper kept singing. Halfway through a favorite tune by Willie Nelson, he suddenly realized two things.

The sun was starting to rise over the horizon and Anthony was finally asleep.

He put the baby back in his crib—thankful for the blinds that kept the room dark—and crept out into the hallway. Grabbing a much-needed cup of coffee and the handheld baby monitor, he headed to the front porch. Fresh air was called for right about now.

He stared out over the land. The buildings and gentle rolling hills that made up Molly's Pride were still dark against the sky that slowly lightened. The quiet of the morning was only punctured by the soft snores coming through the baby monitor.

Damn, maybe he wasn't doing the right thing after all.

Yeah, they'd made it through the night, but what if he was wrong? What if Anthony cried for so long because he was sick and had only worn himself out?

Stretching his arms wide, Cooper worked out the kinks in his back while offering a silent prayer that this crazy parenting plan of his was the right thing to do.

"I'll take anything you want to send me," he said to the heavens, resting one shoulder against the porch landing. "Just give me a sign."

Ignoring his coffee, he stared into the distance, watching as dark shadows gave way to the coming daylight, a slow and easy progression that never failed to lift his spirits. Then on the horizon a cloud of dust formed out of nowhere, coming straight at him at breakneck speed. The sound of pounding horse hooves filled the air.

The cloud moved closer, taking the shape of a horse and rider. He straightened the moment the chestnut-colored quarter horse, recognizable by its well-muscled body and powerful, rounded hindquarters, galloped in front of the cottage.

The rider was a woman. She rode without a saddle, crouched low on the horse's back, at ease and in control, with only the reins of the bridle in her grip. Her white dress billowed behind her, molding her curves and displaying miles of long lean legs. Her hair carelessly whipped in the wind, mimicking the horse's tail in length and dark color.

Well, I'll be damned.

He stepped off the porch, the morning dew soaking through his socks, and watched her ride to the top of a nearby hill. The horse slowed to a stop. The rider straightened and turned as if she felt him watching her.

A bright shaft of sunshine had him shielding his eyes. He stepped into the shadow near the porch railing, but when he dropped his hand, she was gone.

Whoa! Who was that beautiful lone rider?

Chapter Two

Cooper listened for the sound of galloping hooves, but heard nothing. The air was still and silent. Then a cool breeze washed over him and he blinked. Hard.

Had he been asleep? Was she a dream?

"Cooper?"

He spun around and found Isabella, JR's wife, behind him.

"Are you all right?" she asked, moving closer. "You seem a little dazed."

Rubbing at his eyes, Cooper shook off the vision of the lady in white and smiled. "Hey, Isabella. No, not dazed, just asleep on my feet, I guess."

She nodded toward the baby monitor on the railing. "Rough first night?"

He shrugged. "We made it through. What are you doing out here so early?"

"Just taking a stroll and enjoying the coolness of

the morning." She tenderly rubbed her rounded abdomen. "Junior tends to be an early riser. Much like his daddy."

"Well, let's hope Anthony doesn't take after either of them." He glanced at his watch, surprised to see how much time had passed since he put his son to bed. "I just got the little guy to fall asleep an hour ago."

As soon as Cooper spoke, a cooing noise came through the monitor.

"Geez, not again."

"Oh, you must be exhausted. I can sit with Anthony if you want to grab a shower or get some sleep yourself."

Cooper hesitated. He probably smelled like a mixture of formula, strained peas and baby powder. A shower would be great, but he wondered if it would get back to Jeremy and Kirsten if he took Isabella up on her offer.

"I'm not here to spy on you, Cooper." Isabella's soft words cut into his thoughts. "And no one is keeping score on your parenting skills. I'll admit I headed this way because I figured the baby would have you up early. I just wanted to see how you two were doing."

He believed the sincerity in her words. "Thanks. It sounds like he's gone back to sleep, but a shower would be great."

Once inside, Isabella waved off his apology for the condition of the kitchen and shooed him toward the back of the cottage.

After checking on once-again-sleeping Anthony, Cooper went into the bathroom in his room, stripped down and stood under the hot spray of the shower.

His mind wandered back to the horse and rider. Had he been hallucinating—who was that beautiful angel?

Tired of the bar scene and rarely in one place longer than a month or so over the last year, it'd been a while since Cooper had been in the company of an unattached lady. Not that his body had forgotten how to respond to the sight of incredible legs and curves to match.

But riding bareback across his cousin's ranch?

He still wasn't sure he hadn't fallen asleep in those few surreal moments, and decided to discover if that vision on horseback had been a figment of his imagination.

Finishing up with a blast of cold water to chase away the final cobwebs, Cooper got out of the shower, dried off and pulled on a pair of jeans and a T-shirt. He walked back into the living room and found Isabella engrossed in his parenting book. He thought about asking her about the mysterious woman, but what if she *had* only been a vision brought on by his exhaustion?

"Interesting stuff, huh?" he asked instead.

She smiled up at him. "Typical reading for a new dad?"

"Especially for one who's only been at it a few weeks." He paused for a moment and then asked, "Do you mind staying just a bit longer? It's been over a week since I've visited Solo. I know JR has had one of the crew members exercising him, but I'd love to take him out for a quick run."

"Sure, go ahead. I'm here as long as you need me."

After making sure she had his cell phone number, Cooper pulled on his boots, grabbed his beat-up straw cowboy hat and headed toward the main barn. He stopped to look at the fresh tracks left in the soft earth by this morning's rider.

So the lady did exist.

Once inside the barn, he took a deep breath, relishing

the familiar smells of horses, leather and hay. It was a scent ingrained in his soul from the first time he'd visited Red Rock as a kid with his brothers and sister. Their mother had shipped them off to stay with her cousin, Ryan Fortune, and his wife, Lily, at the Fortune family homestead so she could travel across Europe with her latest boyfriend. Of all the places at the Double Crown Ranch, Cooper had loved the horse stables the best.

He greeted Solo with a fresh carrot, but his friend seemed more excited about the prospect of taking his owner for a ride than the treat. He quivered with anticipation as Cooper saddled him. When they cleared the fenced corral, the buckskin stallion took off from the gentle trot to a high-speed gallop.

Moments later, they left the buildings behind and it was only a man, his horse and the wild open Texas countryside. Cooper slowed the animal and found himself searching the rolling hills and flatlands for any sign of the beauty in white he'd seen just over an hour ago.

Nothing.

Disappointed, he turned back. He needed time to give Solo a proper rubdown before returning to Anthony. Maybe later he would bring his son out to the barn to meet the horse. He liked the idea of someday teaching the boy how to ride.

He walked the horse back to the barn to allow him to cool down. Once inside, he gave his buddy a full brushing and started to put the supplies back when he heard—

Singing?

Light, feminine and slightly off-key. He followed the lyrical voice, until finally in the first stall, he found her.

His angel.

Only now her curves were covered by jeans and a simple white T-shirt with the name of the ranch, and well-used, low-heeled boots on her feet. She was a beauty, the natural kind, her long dark hair now pulled back in a high ponytail with loose strands brushing her forehead. An inner glow seemed to radiate from her as she sang softly to the chestnut horse—the same one he'd seen her riding this morning.

He opened his mouth, but his mind blanked on the usual flirting he'd perfected to an art form. Confused by the sudden loss of words, he leaned against the stall door and enjoyed the view.

She moved with purpose and a sureness of someone who'd been around horses all her life. Her touch was gentle, her focus completely on the animal she tended. Moving to the horse's head, she met the animal's broad flat forehead with her own and finished her tune with a gentle kiss.

And damn if a small part of Cooper's heart didn't fall head over boot heels for her. The feeling was so foreign, he couldn't name it and refused to even try.

He gave his head a quick shake to dispel the crazy notion and crossed his arms over his chest. Thankful when his brain finally engaged, he said the first thing that came to his mind. "Did it hurt when you fell from heaven?"

Kelsey Hunt froze at the masculine voice. From where she stood she couldn't see a face, only a pair of well-worn jeans and cowboy boots that looked as broken in as her own.

Had JR hired another stable hand? In the last year, her boss had turned Molly's Pride into a bustling ranch with new help starting every week. Having come home to Red Rock and this job eight months ago, she was already considered an old hand.

Might as well set this Romeo straight.

"Sorry, cowboy, but the stall is freshly cleaned of manure. I won't allow you to drop any more in here with pick-up lines like that."

She offered a wink to her horse, Harley, and she could've sworn the mare winked right back. Having her heart broken not once, not twice, but three times in the last decade was enough to convince her that the no-strings-attached approach was the best. Her life was about the four-legged creatures she understood with a spooky clarity.

Men? Forget it.

"That bad, huh?"

His raspy chuckle caused a ripple through her insides so intense it actually made her knees weaken for a moment. She chalked up the reaction to her inability to get enough sleep the night before, a rarity for her as she worked hard and slept harder. For some reason, she'd spent hours tossing and turning, leading her to impulsively take a ride at dawn. In her nightgown, no less.

She walked to the end of her horse, smoothing her hand down the glossy coat as she went. Might as well look this guy in the eye and let him know they were coworkers and nothing more. "Believe it or not, I've heard…w-worse."

She cleared her throat, blaming the catch in her voice on the dryness of fresh hay she'd just put out for Harley. That had to be it. It couldn't be because of the intensity in the cowboy's chocolate-brown eyes as he stared at her.

He wasn't overly tall, just shy of six feet and he filled out his T-shirt nicely with wide shoulders and muscular arms that came from hard work. The straw Stetson had seen better days, but he wore it as naturally as if he'd been born in it. His faded jeans fit him like a second skin.

His gaze slowly traveled the length of her, too, but she didn't feel annoyed as she often did by a man's stare. Maybe because there wasn't any unseemly suggestion in his eyes, just warm appreciation with a hint of—

Wariness? Now, that was odd for a flirty cowboy.

She swallowed hard before she spoke. "It's best if I make it clear right now. I don't play where I sleep."

That brought his attention back to her face. "Excuse me?"

"What I mean is, I don't get involved with the people I work with. In my experience, mixing business with pleasure can be toxic, so it's best to nip things in the bud right up front."

"I'll keep that in mind considering I don't work here." He pushed himself away from the stall door. "Cooper Fortune."

Another Fortune? The town of Red Rock was crawling with them. He wasn't one of JR's brothers—those she knew by sight—so he must be a cousin. Is that why the name sounded so familiar?

"Wait, you belong to Solo."

He grinned, his smile rising into one dimple. "That's an interesting way of putting it. I prefer to think of him and me as buds, belonging to each other."

She blushed. "I'm sorry. I just naturally pair up

the human with their animal instead of the other way around. Professional habit."

"And what profession is that?"

"Horse trainer. I'm in charge of the equine program here at Molly's Pride. I'm Kelsey Hunt."

He took a step forward but stopped short of entering the stall. One hand stretched outward. "It's good to meet you, Kelsey."

Because it would've been rude not to, she placed her hand in his. Calloused fingers spoke of hard work as much as his tanned, weathered skin spoke of a life lived outdoors. She tried to remember if JR had told her anything about the owner of the beautiful stallion they'd been housing for the last couple of weeks, but nothing came to mind.

"Are you in town for a visit, Mr. Fortune?"

He released her when she pulled away. "The name is Cooper and I'm here for more than a visit. I'm moving back to Red Rock. Permanently, I guess."

She tucked Harley's grooming brush and mane comb on a nearby shelf and grabbed her ball cap with the ranch's logo. "You guess?"

"JR and his gang of brothers are my cousins. My brother, Ross, and sister, Frannie, live here, too." He answered while backing up, allowing her to leave the stall and closed the door behind her. "And my son is here as well."

He was married.

And here he was handing out pick-up lines. Geez, she felt like a loser. One would think with her history she would be able to spot a married man by now.

His slow drawl about "falling from heaven" had been a line if ever she heard one. She prayed he wasn't another cowboy who figured whatever happened in the barn was okay as long as the little woman in the main house didn't find out. She loved her job, but fighting off one of her boss's rich relatives wasn't part of her job description.

Tugging on the cap, she pulled her long ponytail through the back keyhole. It was time to start her work-day. This cowboy didn't seem to be in any hurry to leave, even though he was checking his watch for a second time.

"Well, I should get to my office."

He shoved his hands in his pockets and looked around the oversize facility. "This is some place you have here. I know JR refurbished the original barn, but this one's brand-new, right?"

Kelsey could tell he was impressed and for some reason, that pleased her. She'd started here with two horses and a brand-new building JR gave her total control over. Her program now housed a dozen finely trained horses that sold for top dollar as well as the horses she'd rescued from neglect.

"Yes, it's just under a year old." She headed toward her office in the front corner of the barn, keeping distance between them as he walked with her. "So, are you and Mrs. Fortune staying here at Molly's Pride?"

"Well, there's plenty of Mrs. Fortunes running around Red Rock, but none belong to me." He stopped at her door when she did, the power of his gaze commanded she look at him. "I'm not married."

For a moment it looked like he wanted to say something else, but he didn't. She grabbed the door handle and pushed with a bit too much force. "Oh, I assumed when said your son…"

Embarrassed, she let her voice trail off as she moved to her desk, oddly relieved to have the two feet of wood between her and this cowboy.

"Anthony and I have—well, we just found each other a couple of weeks ago." He stood in the open doorway, again not invading her space, and punched at the frame with his fist. Not hard, but there was a hint of frustration behind the controlled action. "His mother and I haven't been involved in over a year and I never knew she was pregnant."

Meaning his son was only an infant. "But you've worked things out it seems, if you're here."

He shook his head. "She died in a car accident around New Year's. My cousin has been taking care of my son until they found—until I found out about him and came home."

Immediately, Kelsey thought of her sister, whose husband had died in a construction accident two years ago. Lost for months, Jessica had finally emerged from her grief-induced haze to realize she was doing just fine raising their four young kids by herself, with a little help from Kelsey and Jessica's parents.

Kelsey sank to her chair and waved at the matching one in front of her desk. The man did look like he needed to sit. "I'm so sorry. That must've been some phone call. I remember reading about that accident... or was it the one involving JR's father that led to him being missing for months? He's your uncle, right?"

Cooper dropped into the chair. "Yes, my mother's brother. I guess there were two eventful accidents back in January. At least William's has a better outcome now that he's been found and is back home again."

Home, but not whole. Everyone in town knew William

Fortune remembered nothing of his previous life. He was back at the Double Crown Ranch with his fiancée, Lily, having gone missing on what was supposed to be their wedding day.

"Well, finding out you're a father must be a happy thing for you."

The cowboy nodded, but the slump of his shoulders revealed an invisible burden. "It's taking some getting used to. I've never been around kids much and rarely one who can barely sit upright. I feel like I've stepped into a parallel universe with strange words like butt cream, binky and onesie."

He suddenly offered her that lopsided grin again and nudged his hat farther on his brow. "Say, you wouldn't happen to know anything about babies, would ya?"

There was such hope in his voice that she found herself suppressing a snort of laughter. "Ah, horse babies, cow babies, even ducklings and piglets are right up my alley. Human babies, no way. That's more my sister's speed."

"So you're not married? No kids?"

The closest she'd come to marriage was years ago when she found an engagement ring hidden in her boyfriend's dresser drawer. Foolishly she'd thought it was meant for her. It wasn't. Every relationship she'd had since had taught her that falling in love meant saying goodbye. No, thanks. She hadn't even had a date since moving back home.

"Nope, I must've been absent the day they were handing out the maternal gene. I have no interest in marriage or kids." An idea suddenly came to her. She grabbed the photograph on her desk and flipped it around. "Now, my sister, Jessica, has the mothering gene down pat. I'll have to introduce you two."

His eyes went from her to the frame image of her sister surrounded by her four kids, all under the age of eight. It lingered there and Kelsey had to fight back the flame of jealousy that licked at her insides.

You aren't interested, remember?

A ready-made family wasn't what Kelsey was looking for. This cowboy certainly wasn't what she was looking for.

Because she wasn't looking.

"Are you trying to fix me up with your sister?" he finally asked, looking back at her with those deep brown eyes of his.

Kelsey swallowed hard against the sudden lump lodged in her throat and pushed the words out of her mouth. "You'd be perfect for each other."

Chapter Three

Cooper wasn't interested in Kelsey's sister.

Still, he wasn't sure if that's where the pretty horse trainer was going with her insistence yesterday that he and Jessica should meet. Heck, he'd been in a brain fog thanks to a lack of sleep and finding out the beautiful woman he'd seen on horseback was real and working right here at Molly's Pride.

A woman who'd quickly put him in his place, he thought with a smile as he watched Anthony snoozing on a quilt in the middle of the living room floor.

After returning from the barn yesterday and thanking Isabella again for watching his son, he'd decided getting some sleep was more important than cleaning the house. It hadn't been as easy as he thought. Every time he closed his eyes he saw Kelsey's long dark hair or her pretty smile.

She'd been so easy to talk to and hadn't seemed upset

about his clumsy attempt at a line. He'd checked out her ring finger, happy to find it empty. He was even happier about her "no dating coworkers" rule. At least that cut down on the competition.

Because he was definitely interested in Kelsey.

So he'd smiled at the "hooking up with her sister" remark and headed back to the cottage. The rest of the day had been relatively uneventful, not counting the handful of phone calls from his siblings and cousins that had interrupted his nap. Obviously, they were all checking up on him. Later, he and Anthony had joined JR and Isabella for dinner. It wasn't hard to get JR to talk about his ranching operations, and Cooper soon learned his cousin thought the world of Kelsey Hunt and her horse-training skills.

He also learned Kelsey lived in an apartment on the second floor of the stables.

Which was why he'd started today with a morning visit to Solo, although he told himself he was only taking Anthony to meet his best friend. The baby had been fascinated with the horse and all the sights and smells of the stables. Cooper held Anthony in his arms, pride filling his chest as the little boy clapped and giggled.

No sign of Kelsey though, so they'd returned home for another bottle and the baby's midmorning nap. Cooper sat nearby, reading the chapter on helping your baby to learn to sit when the cell phone attached to his hip vibrated. He rose from the chair and went into the kitchen.

"Hello?"

"Cooper? It's Lily Fortune."

Lily was his Uncle William's fiancée, but she was also a Fortune having been married to William's cousin,

Ryan, until his death years ago of brain cancer. William had lost his beloved wife a few years later, but now William and Lily had fallen in love and had planned to marry.

But William had disappeared on their wedding day.

"Hi, Lily." He wondered how she got his phone number. "Is everything okay? Is it Uncle William?"

"Oh, no, sweetie, William is…fine. His memory and his emotional state, or lack thereof on both accounts, are the same."

Lily's unsteady voice filled his ear. She then paused to take in a deep breath before she continued. "He's calmer now and seems more at home here on the ranch with each passing day." She sounded calmer now herself. "I'm sorry if I worried you by calling."

Cooper released the breath he hadn't even realized he'd been holding. "Ah, no, that's fine. What's up?"

"I heard about you moving out on your own with the baby, and I wondered if there was anything you needed? Is there anything I can do for you?"

Lily Fortune was an amazing woman. She ran the Double Crown Ranch and chaired numerous charities supported by the Fortune Foundation, all while doing her best to help the man she loved regain his memories—of his family, and the life they'd planned to live together.

He found himself wishing he'd been lucky enough to have this lady for a mother instead of the self-centered woman who probably had no idea that she had another grandchild living here in Red Rock.

"Thanks, but we're doing fine." Cooper peeked around the doorway to check on his son. "It's a pretty steep learning curve, but I think I'm getting the hang of it."

"Of course you are. I don't have any doubt you'll be a terrific father."

Her words had him standing a bit taller. "Thank you, Lily. You know, I was planning to come out and visit the ranch soon, but Jeremy recommended we not overload William with too many visitors at once."

"Oh, you're welcome anytime. I can't say for sure what kind of mood your uncle will be in. Sometimes he's fine and other times he's a bit cranky, but I think that's frustration more than anything else."

They spoke for a few more minutes, but then Anthony started to fuss. Cooper ended the call, having learned his son tended to wake up fast and loud.

"Easy there, partner." He looked at the baby lying flat on his back, arms and legs flailing. "No need to get all excited."

Anthony didn't agree because he let loose a howling cry just as a knock sounded from the door.

Cooper picked him up and the smell and weight of Anthony's diaper told him exactly why the kid was upset. "Whew, you stink!"

The knock came again, and he went to answer, mentally cringing as he hefted the baby into his arms, the diaper flattening against his forearm. He opened the door to find Kelsey standing on his front porch, wearing the same outfit he'd seen her in yesterday.

He appreciated the curves beneath her clingy T-shirt and snug-fitting jeans. A ball cap shaded her eyes and her hair was once again pulled up in a ponytail. He was suddenly struck with an urge to see her hair down around her shoulders. Naked shoulders would be even better, as she leaned over him—

A softly cleared throat caught his attention, and he noticed a pretty lady standing next to Kelsey. They looked so much alike, he knew instantly they were related. The three little kids with them told him she must be Kelsey's sister.

Boy, she really was serious about her matchmaking.

He didn't know if he should be amused or bothered that Kelsey had brought her widowed sister, kids in tow, over to meet him.

Had he been the only one to pick up on the instant connection they'd shared yesterday? A connection that had him opening up to a perfect stranger about how much his life had changed in the last month?

"Hey there. Hope we're not catching you at a bad time," Kelsey said, a smile gracing her kissable lips.

Yeah, perfect.

"Ah, no." Cooper patted Anthony's bottom lightly, sending tiny bursts of a foul odor into the air as if to punctuate where his priorities needed to lie. His nose wrinkled. "The little guy just woke from a nap and I was heading off to do diaper duty."

"Don't let us stop you," the other woman said with a smile. "He'll probably be happier once he's clean and dry."

"Well, come on in—" Cooper stepped back "—and make yourselves at home. I'll be right back."

He hustled to the baby's room and laid a still-crying Anthony on the changing table. Replacing the messy diaper took longer than he planned. Boy, who knew a body as tiny as this could put out so much...stuff.

Finally done, he put a new one-piece sleeper on Anthony, noting the dwindling supply of baby wipes seemed to be in direct correlation to the dirty laundry filling the nearby hamper. Looked like a trip to the grocery store was next on his list.

Despite a fresh diaper, Anthony was testing the capacity of his lungs as Cooper walked back into the living room.

"I'm sorry," he said, raising his voice to be heard over Anthony's crying as he patted his son's back. "He must've realized he'd nodded off earlier without finishing his bottle."

"Here, let me take him." Kelsey's sister plucked Anthony out of his arms and turned to her children. "Kids, park yourselves on the sofa and find something in your backpacks to keep you busy while your Aunt Kelsey and I get to know this adorable little thing."

Dumbfounded, Cooper stood there as Anthony stopped his crying and gazed up at the woman as the children scrambled to do their mother's bidding.

"Wow." He finally found his voice, but the single syllable was the best he could come up with. "That's... wow."

"Cooper Fortune, your son's kidnapper is my sister, Jessica Hunt-Myers." Kelsey made the quick introduction. "Jessica, this is Cooper Fortune."

"Hi, there," Jessica said. "I think I can keep—ah, what's his name?"

"Anthony."

"I think I can keep Anthony busy for a few minutes if you want to make him that bottle." Jessica sat in the chair Cooper had vacated and easily bounced the baby on her lap while answering three different questions from three different kids.

Cooper moved into the kitchen and quickly made a new bottle. He returned to the living room, expecting Jessica to give up her claim to his son, but she just motioned for the bottle, popping it into Anthony's mouth.

He moved to the matching chair and sat, his gaze drawn to Kelsey. Perched on the end of the couch, with the youngest of her sister's kids on her lap, she pointed to something in the book the little boy held. His tiny eyebrows puckered in concentration for a minute before he clucked like a chicken.

Cooper grinned. "Hey, that's pretty good. Can you do a cow?"

The little boy looked at him. "We're not at that page yet."

"Adam." His mother admonished him with one word, before she turned to Cooper. "I'm sorry, I didn't introduce my children. The little one is Adam and he's a very precocious three, and the twins, Braden and Bethany, are four. My oldest, Ella, is seven, so she's at school."

"What's per-cos-ick?" Adam asked his mother.

"Precocious, and it means you're very smart," she answered with a smile as she set aside the empty bottle to lift Anthony to her shoulder. "All of my children are very smart," she added when the twins started to protest. "They take after their father."

"Kelsey told me about your husband. I'm sorry."

Cooper watched as sadness flickered across the woman's face before she offered him a smile.

"Thank you. She told me about Anthony's mother. I'm sorry, too. You must have your hands full learning to be a single parent." She patted the baby's back, and soon Anthony let out a loud burp and giggled at his accomplishment. "I know what that's like. If you need any help, just give me a holler."

He turned to look at Kelsey, who seemed very interested in the picture book her nephew was holding. So, she really was serious about this matchmaking.

Hmm, right idea, wrong sister.

Cooper glanced back at Jessica. "I'll keep that in mind."

"Are you sure?" Kelsey stared at her sister over the roof of her car. "You really want to do *this*?"

"Are you kidding?" Jessica shot back as she shut her door and activated the automatic locks. "You have no idea how much I am going to enjoy myself."

They walked across the parking lot toward the large building. Seconds later, automatic doors swished open and then closed behind them, locking out the Texas heat and bathing them in a cool breeze.

"With Mom and Dad watching the kids this afternoon, I've got three hours all to myself."

Kelsey followed Jessica as she ventured farther into the brightly lit entrance. "So, go see a movie, get a massage, read a book…anything but this."

"Spoken like a single woman who can be in and out of here in less than fifteen minutes and use the express checkout line."

Jessica grabbed a large silver cart and aimed it toward the rainbow of colors that made up the produce section of the super-size grocery store. "Now, I can thump melons to my heart's content, wrangle between cuts of meats at the butcher shop and actually make good use of my overstuffed coupon caddy."

Kelsey rolled her eyes as Jessica's fingers lightly danced over the vibrant array of apples, from light green to deep red, piled in front of her.

"This is nirvana," her sister said.

They moved to the first aisle and Kelsey grabbed a bottle of wine from the end display and put it in the cart. A six-pack cellophane package of chocolate bars followed next.

She caught her sister's disapproving glance. "Hey, you have your idea of heaven and I have mine."

"Speaking of heaven," Jessica paused as she looked over a selection of breakfast cereals in the next aisle, "that cowboy of yours is pretty dreamland-worthy."

"He's not my cowboy," Kelsey protested. "In fact, I thought the two of you got along famously yesterday."

"Yes, so famously that the guy could barely take his eyes off you the whole time."

"Oh, please."

"Besides, I told you before, I'm not in the market for a replacement for Peter."

Her sister's words were soft, but Kelsey heard the catch in her voice. "I've never suggested you replace him. That would be impossible. I just thought you'd finally turned the corner..."

"I have." Jessica turned to Kelsey and gave her arm a gentle squeeze. "My life is filled with my children and my art. There's no room right now for a man."

"But you could fall in love again—"

"I h-had my shot at hap-happily ever after," Jessica interrupted, her own words stumbling from her lips. "And it was wonderful for the short time it lasted."

Her sister's sudden interest in spaghetti sauce and the rapid blinking told Kelsey to change the subject.

Jessica took care of that for her as she grabbed the same brand of sauce she'd used for years and put it in the cart. "Now you, on the other hand—"

"Aren't interested."

Jessica looked her in the eye. "Liar."

"Okay, so Cooper Fortune is a total hottie," Kelsey relented, knowing it was useless to argue. She hated that her sister had always been able to tell when she was being less than honest. "But he and that adorable baby have got home and family written all over them and that's not for me."

"Yeah, I've heard you sing that tune for a long time. Ever since that jerk you dated all through college dumped you just before graduation for that former Miss Texas who could give him the proper home and proper children." Jessica punctuated her last words with the two quick jerks of her fingers showing she was quoting Kelsey's ex's words.

"Well, he was right. Thomas is doing very well in his law practice and he's eyeing a political future. He and his family made the cover of *Texas Now!* a few months ago."

"Whoopee."

"Besides, he never liked that I smelled like a barn at the end of the day." Something he failed to mention even once during their four-year relationship after they met their freshman year at West Texas A&M University.

"An issue I don't think Cooper would have a problem with."

Kelsey grabbed a package of cookies from the shelf and placed them in the cart. "Been there, done that. My last two relationships were both with cowboys and neither one ended pretty."

"Not surprising since you didn't bring either of them home to Red Rock to meet the family."

She'd tried, but neither cowboy had had any interest in her life back here while she was dating them, which turned out to be a good thing as both men ended up walking out on her. "Well, my only focus right now is building one of the best equine programs Red Rock has ever seen."

"You're kicking butt and your boss knows it, but that doesn't mean all men—or all cowboys, for that matter— need to be off-limits. Cooper Fortune is perfect—" Jessica turned the corner and started past the next aisle, then stopped. "Hmm, it looks like perfect cowboy is having a problem at the moment."

Kelsey didn't know what her sister was talking about until she noticed Cooper, standing in the middle of the baby aisle, a confused look on his handsome face as he held up two different jumbo-size packages of diapers. The shopping cart in front of him was full while his son dozed in the attached car seat.

A burst of fiery attraction exploded in her gut, but she quickly put it out in hopes that Jess might just find herself drawn to the man. That thought gave Kelsey another kick in her stomach—and it wasn't a pleasant one.

The last time the two of them took a liking to the same guy was back in junior high school when Kelsey found herself crushing on a boy who ended up taking Jessica to the eighth-grade dance. The same boy her sister dated all through high school and married at the tender age of nineteen. Peter and Jessica had always only had eyes for each other, so it'd been easy for Kelsey to let go of her silly case of puppy love.

Not that she liked Cooper Fortune.

Not like that. Yeah, he was the quintessential hunky Texas cowboy, but again, she wasn't interested.

Remember that, girlfriend. Not interested.

"Oh, the poor guy." Jessica turned her cart. "Come on, let's help him."

Kelsey silently repeated her words as she followed her sister's lead, noticing the fine way Cooper's shoulders filled out his faded, snap-front shirt, the sleeves rolled up to reveal strong forearms.

"You're looking a bit lost, cowboy," Jessica said, stopping her cart next to his. "Need any help? This is probably the most confusing aisle in the entire store."

Her sister's words pulled Kelsey from her thoughts in time to see the bewilderment on Cooper's face fade into an easygoing smile.

"You're not kidding." He dropped his hands, the diapers bouncing off his jean-clad legs. "It took me ten minutes to figure out which baby wipes were the right ones and I haven't even hit the food area yet."

His dark eyes looked past her sister and latched on to her. His laid-back grin deepened as he added a hint of sexiness to it. "Hey, Kelsey."

The image of her kissing that mouth while slowly pulling open his shirt—*snap, snap, snap*—filled Kelsey's head. It took a hard blink to erase it. Her mouth was suddenly drier than a Texas summer day and she had to lick her lips before she spoke. "Hey, yourself."

He held her gaze for a moment before dropping his eyes to her lips. She could've sworn he actually knew what she'd been thinking, as impossible as that might be.

"So…" Jessica cleared her throat. "Are you a bit puzzled by the diaper selection?"

Cooper looked at her again, his easy smile back in place. "It's that obvious, huh? I didn't even think to write down the brand my cousin and his fiancée had used for the little guy and we ran out this morning."

Jessica pointed to the package in his right hand. "Those always worked best for my crowd, but you need the right size."

"Size?"

"It's based on the baby's weight."

"Oh." Cooper looked at the packages, put both back on the shelf and grabbed three in the correct size. "Anthony is going through these things like crazy. Better safe than sorry. Now, it's on to that amazing assortment of baby mush—ah, food."

"Jess, why don't you lend your expertise on that, too?" Kelsey grabbed her sister's cart and pushed it past Cooper's to allow another shopper to get by. "I can keep working on your list for you."

Jessica shot Kelsey a frown over Cooper's bent form as he shoved the diapers onto the bottom shelf of his cart. "Sure, I can do that."

Kelsey only grinned in return and forced herself not to look at Cooper's perfect backside, encased in faded denim. "Great, where's your list?"

"Could I bother you to keep an eye on Anthony instead for a few minutes?" Cooper rose and turned to her, moving closer while gesturing toward the baby. "He's been trying to nap since we arrived. Every time I move the cart it wakes him."

"Uh, yeah…" She had to tip her head back to look at him, and she could've sworn the tips of his boots scraped hers, he was that close. "Sure, it's no bother."

Damn, that sexier-than-sin smile was back and directed right at her. "Thanks, I'll owe you."

Cooper and Jessica moved toward the other end of the aisle where the stacks of baby food jars stood in precise rows on the shelves. Kelsey looked down at Anthony, watching his tiny eyelids flutter as he slept. With his dark brown hair, and the brown eyes she'd seen briefly yesterday at the cottage, he looked a lot like his daddy.

He'd fallen asleep in Jessica's arms yesterday, the two of them the exact likeness of Madonna and child. If there was anyone who'd been destined to be a mother, it was her sister. From childhood, she'd been a loving mama to her baby dolls while Kelsey's side of the room had been filled with horse figurines.

"Looks like we both got what we wanted," Kelsey whispered, unable to stop herself from stroking the baby's soft cheek. "Except Jessica never planned on being a single parent. That's why your daddy and she would be such a good match."

Anthony chose that moment to open his eyes, and as if he wasn't happy with her idea, started to fuss.

Kelsey jerked her hand away and looked for Cooper. He and Jessica were at the other end of the aisle. The baby's fidgeting intensified, his eyes now clenched tightly closed, so she grabbed the cart and started to push it back and forth, but that only increased his crying.

Geez, it was moments like this when she usually gave her niece or nephew back to their mother. Another quick glance told her Jessica and Cooper weren't heading back to this end of the aisle soon, so she quickly unbuckled the baby and hefted him into her arms.

"Okay, no need to get upset," she cooed while rubbing the baby's back. "I've got you."

Anthony snuggled into her shoulder and she held tighter, tucking her face close to his and continuing with her soft words. Her body moved in a natural swaying motion, and soon she was rewarded when the baby heaved a deep sigh and fell back asleep, his breath coming in gentle puffs against her neck.

"Well, you certainly seem to have the magic touch."

Kelsey turned to find Cooper standing behind her. Jessica and her shopping cart had disappeared. How'd that happen? And how was it that she and Cooper were the only people in this vast aisle of the grocery store?

"Anthony looks right at home in your arms," he added, taking a step closer, trapping her between the cart and the shelves behind her. "Not that I blame him. Envy, maybe. You know, I think you might be wrong about lacking the maternal instinct."

"Oh, no. Jessica is—"

"An amazing lady and from what I've seen, a terrific mom." Cooper cut off her words while reaching out to gently tug on a loose strand of hair that had fallen from her ponytail. "But she's not the sister who's caught my attention. You are."

Chapter Four

As far as dirty diapers went, this one had to be the world record holder. Cooper choked back his gag reflex when the pungent odor filled his nose and mouth.

Anthony looked up at him and smiled.

Cooper's heart gave a little kick as he peeled off the baby's messy clothes and set them to one side of the quilt. So much for having done two loads of laundry this morning.

"Damn, this is nasty!" He ripped at the diaper tabs and pulled the front flap back, and the nausea factor climbed a hundredfold as his eyes burned. "Whew! Major nasty!"

Anthony giggled.

"Glad you think this is so funny." Cooper grimaced, grabbing a handful of baby wipes. He tried to clean up his son, but all he seemed to do was succeed in spreading the mess even farther. He removed the diaper and dropped it on an old issue of "Texas Now!" he'd been reading. "Boy, you need to be hosed down to get rid of this stench."

"I second that."

On his hands and knees, Cooper turned and looked over his shoulder. Kelsey stood peering at him through the screen door.

"It looks like I got here just in time." She hoisted the blue plastic object in her hands a bit higher. "My sister said she offered you this baby tub while in the store. Can I come in?"

"If you think your nose can stand it." Cooper found himself grinning at her. "And your timing is perfect."

"Why don't we try rinsing him off before you get him in a bath?" Kelsey suggested as she walked into the dining area and placed the tub on the table. She unzipped her hoodie and peeled it off her shoulders revealing yet another ranch T-shirt, this time pale pink in color. "Is the bathroom sink big enough?"

Big enough for what?

Cooper tore his gaze from her body and shook his head, realizing she was talking about the baby. "No, and the kitchen sink is too big. He squirms so much that I can't keep a good grip on him, which is why your sister made her generous offer."

"Okay, give me a minute to get everything we need. Then you can get that stinky baby washed up."

"Make it a fast minute, okay?" Cooper grabbed the soiled onesie and put it over Anthony's privates. He'd already been a victim of the baby's sudden need to urinate, diaper or not, resulting in a steady stream hitting him square in the chest. "I'm about to lose my lunch over here."

Kelsey's laugh followed her down the hall to the baby's room. The low, sexy sound rocked Cooper back on his heels. Two days ago, he'd been tempted beyond reason to kiss her in the baby aisle of the grocery store.

Despite the craziness of their current situation, he found himself ready to do it again. And this time he wouldn't back away.

Kelsey had been so focused on Anthony that day, her head bent, humming a low tune as she rocked him, that she hadn't heard him and Jessica approach. Her sister had given him a sly wink as she disappeared around the corner with her own shopping cart. Moments later, he had Kelsey cornered between the cart and the shelving. The silky feeling of her hair sliding through his fingers, the softness of her cheek, the way her lips parted in surprise when he made it clear she was the one he wanted.

And he did want her.

It'd been over a year since he'd been with a woman. His self-imposed celibacy had surprised him, but no woman had stirred his interest. Not like Kelsey had from the first moment he'd seen her racing across the ranch on horseback.

Cooper yanked his shirt free from his jeans, letting the material hang loose. The last thing he needed was her seeing his body's response to the thoughts running through his head.

Because he'd read fear in her eyes that afternoon in the store. Oh, there'd been flashes of desire, too, but he wasn't sure if getting mixed up with her, no matter how his blood pulsed with a steady longing, was the best idea.

Not with the little guy in front of him as his number one priority.

"Okay, I think I got everything." She walked back into the living room, her arms filled with bottles and towels.

Putting the stuff on the table, she disappeared into the kitchen. Seconds later, he heard cabinets being opened before she joined him with two garbage bags, quickly disposing of the offending diaper, the magazine it sat on and the pile of used wipes. She motioned for him to lift Anthony. He did and she slid the soiled quilt out from under him and stuck it in the other bag.

"Ah, you're learning pretty quickly, huh?" She grinned and pointed to the outfit still covering the baby's lower half.

"Once was enough." Cooper returned her smile. "Now I keep him covered...just in case."

She took care of the two bags as Cooper stood. He watched her lay a large towel on the dining room table and fill the tub with soapy water, making sure the water wasn't too warm.

"You've done this before," he said.

"Not for a long time. I was around to help with Jessica's oldest daughter, Ella, but I'd only come back to visit when the others were born until I moved back to Red Rock last year." She placed the tub on the towel. "Besides, common sense goes a long way. Come on, I'll help you get that...stuff off him before it dries."

Cooper moved to the sink and held the baby firmly beneath the arms while Kelsey repeatedly doused Anthony's stomach, backside and legs with warm water. They managed to rinse him off with a minimum amount of splashing.

That changed when Cooper transferred the baby to the tub. Having still not mastered the ability to sit up on his own, Anthony didn't let that stop him from kicking at the bubbles or reaching for the tiny washcloth floating on the water.

"Whoa," Cooper cried out. "You're a slippery little sucker!"

He reached for one chubby arm while Kelsey took hold of the other, the two of them getting wrapped up in each other as Anthony's churning feet sent up a shower of bubbles and water.

"I guess he thinks we should be as wet as he is," Kelsey said with a quick laugh. "Here, hold him like this—"

Cooper laughed, too. "Wait, let me get my hand under here—"

"Maybe it would work if I moved over here…"

Kelsey squeezed between him and the table. Cooper sucked in a quick breath as her backside brushed across his crotch. The contact had him bowing his body to keep her from realizing how quickly he was losing the battle to tamp down his reaction, but that only succeeded in dropping his head so it was level with hers.

Anthony chose that moment to let loose with another squeal of happiness and his little feet sent up a second spray of water and bubbles—right into Kelsey's face.

She sputtered and turned away, her ponytail whacking Cooper in the face. "Oops! Sorry about that."

She quickly turned back and they both stilled.

Cooper's gaze locked with hers, his mouth hovering inches from the pouty pink lips that had haunted his dreams. He dropped his head an inch, then paused and drew in a deep breath. A warm and natural scent that spoke of horses, hay and the sweetness of fresh straw-berries filled his head. A scent that matched Kelsey perfectly. A low moan of approval started deep in his chest, but he managed to keep it from escaping.

At least he thought so until her beautiful chocolate-brown eyes grew wide.

"Any idea where we go from here?" she asked.

He had a few suggestions, most of which ended hori-zontal and skin to skin.

As if she could read his thoughts, Kelsey bit down on her lower lip. Damn, he wanted to soothe that bite with a quick swipe of his tongue before he swept it into her mouth—

"Why don't I head to this side of the table?" Kelsey scooted out from under his arms, moving toward the end of the tub but still holding firmly to Anthony. "This way you can get him washed and keep an eye on those unruly legs of his."

Cooper gave his head a quick shake, trying to rid his brain of the erotic images so he could concentrate on his son. "Good idea. It looks like he's got a great future as an All-American punter—"

The soapy washcloth landed on Cooper's chest with a loud splat. Surprised, he grabbed it before it fell to the floor.

"Or maybe an All-American pitcher? I hear the Rang-ers are always looking for someone who can throw a curve like that."

Kelsey's saucy grin went straight to his gut, bursting into a fireball of longing before the blaze quickly moved south. Not good.

Cooper tore his gaze from her to look at Anthony, who

clapped happily at his antics before aiming his bubble-covered fists to his mouth. "Oh, no, you don't."

He reached for the baby's hands with one of his. At the same time he reached behind his neck and with one yank, pulled his soaked shirt up and over his head. Shrugging out one arm, then the other without bothering to undo any of the buttons, he dropped the damp material to the floor.

"That evens the playing field," he said. "Now, let's see if we can get you cleaned up before you flood the house, young man."

Kelsey tried to breathe.

Honest, she did, but the air lodged in her throat refusing to move. It wasn't until Cooper's fingers slipped over hers where she held Anthony in place that her breath finally rushed from her lungs.

He looked at her, but she managed to focus her attention on the soapy water. Of course, that put his perfect six-pack right in her line of sight.

Yowza!

Being a native Texan meant she'd seen plenty of sexy cowboys with tightly toned bodies, but she'd never been affected like this before, by any man. Tanned flesh pulled taut over defined muscles. Muscles that represented strength and years spent outdoors doing hard work.

She found herself inhaling deeply to catch her breath, but it only brought in the clean scent of baby wash and man. A heady combination. As heady as the moment she'd found herself pressed against him when they were wrangling for control of the baby. It had only lasted a moment, but she'd felt the telling hardness against her backside and it'd taken all her willpower not to lean into him. Seconds later she could've sworn he was going to kiss her—

"Ah, Kelsey?"

Her eyes flew to his. A grin told her he'd caught her gawking. That and the bright flash of passion in his eyes caused heat to flood her cheeks. "Y-yes?"

"You can let go now."

"Huh?"

Cooper slid his hands under hers to take hold of Anthony beneath his armpits. "I'm done with the bath. If you could give him a quick rinse while I keep him steady—"

"Yes—of course."

Kelsey released the baby to grab the cup floating in the separate clean water basin. She waited until Cooper lifted his son from the water, tiny feet still churning, sending a spray of bubbles all over Cooper's chest. He sucked in his stomach and his jeans slipped down another inch from his slim hips. A sliver of pale skin appeared, a sharp contrast to the deeply tanned skin everywhere else.

Double yowza!

"Geez, maybe he's destined to be an Olympic swimmer with these restless feet," Cooper said, then grinned. "Let's do this fast…just in case he feels the need to— you know."

Kelsey dragged her attention from Cooper to focus on Anthony, pouring cupful after cupful over the baby's shoulders until he was squeaky clean.

She then grabbed a nearby towel and stepped in close to wrap it around the baby. Cooper mirrored her movements and they again became a tangle of hands and arms and bodies. His hands brushed over her breasts as he cradled his son to his chest, trapping her hands between the fluff of the towel and his heated skin.

"I've got him." Cooper repeated his words from earlier, this time they were said in a hoarse whisper. "You can let go."

She pulled her hands free and stepped back. Cooper's gaze dropped from her face to her body before he blinked hard and turned away.

"Give me a few minutes to get him dressed. Be right back."

To stop herself from watching Cooper's wide back, narrow waist and sexy butt disappear down the hall, Kelsey grabbed the baby's tub and emptied it in the sink.

She rinsed it out and set it outside on the front porch to dry. Then she washed out the baby's dirty onesie using dish soap and rolled it in a towel to soak up the excess moisture. It took her longer to wipe up the rest of the kitchen as soapy water seemed to be everywhere.

Done, she glanced down at herself, noticing for the first time the transparency of her damp T-shirt. Oh, perfect. Cooper would come back any second, probably after stopping off to get a clean, dry shirt of his own, and here she looked like a reject from a wet T-shirt contest.

Would he think it was on purpose?

He was attracted to her, heck, he'd come right out and told her so two days ago. And what had she done in return? Placed his son in his arms, told him she wasn't interested and took off.

Liar, liar, pants on fire.

The childhood taunt rang in her ears as she whipped

off her shirt, thankful for the sports bra she wore on a daily basis, and grabbed her hoodie from the table. Yanking it on, she managed to get the zipper feed into the catch when a male voice stopped her.

"Don't get dressed on my account."

Kelsey looked up.

No clean shirt, no baby. Just one hundred percent, mouth-watering—her eyes dipped—aroused cowboy.

"Cooper."

He crossed the room in a heartbeat, swore softly under his breath before his mouth captured hers in a searing kiss. There was no hesitation, no shyness, no tentatively getting to know the shape of each other's mouths. His lips were firm, his tongue insistent as he swept it into her mouth, seeking, wanting.

She wound her hands around his neck, meeting his kiss head-on, pressing her curves to the hard planes of his chest. His hands brushed her sweat jacket from her shoulders. He broke free of her mouth, his lips moving along to her jaw until he nipped at her ear.

"I wasn't going to do this," he whispered hotly, "but you said my name…"

She arched her neck to give him more access to continue whatever he was doing with his mouth. "Cooper…"

"Yeah, just like that."

His hands sprayed wide across her back, moving from the stretchy fabric of her sports bra, down to the waistband of her jeans until they cupped her backside. He gave a gentle squeeze and pulled her even closer as his mouth took possession of hers again.

She moaned and dug her fingers into the thickness of his hair, wanting him closer, wanting to be closer.

Suddenly, the floor disappeared beneath her feet as Cooper lifted her up against his chest. She hooked her legs around his waist as he walked into the living room, stopping when they reached the couch.

"Anthony," she gasped.

"Fast asleep before I even got the diaper on him."

Cooper let go of her and her boots slid to the carpet. Then he turned and dropped to the cushioned surface, pulling her onto his lap. She straddled him, pressing the most intimate part of herself against his arousal.

Their mutual groans disappeared as they kissed again, her fingers digging into his shoulders as his hands clenched her hips. The center seam of her jeans pressed into the heated dampness between her legs.

Could Cooper feel that heat? Did he have any idea how the urgent rocking of his hips was driving her crazy?

His hands moved upward until he palmed her breasts through the thin fabric of her bra. She responded to his touch by arching her back. He broke free from her mouth and leaned forward. Replacing his hands with his lips, he nipped at one extended nipple right through her bra. At the same time, his free hand went to the juncture of her thighs and the simple pressure of his thumb had her rising up on her knees.

She raked her hands down his chest, her blunt nails scoring his skin. When she reached the hard length of his erection, she cupped him and squeezed. He must've taken that move as an invitation, because he quickly unbuttoned her jeans and lowered the zipper.

Kelsey knew where this was heading, and deep inside she also knew it would be wonderful. Wild and free— that's what she claimed to be, as untamed and liberated as her precious horses. So why couldn't she take this moment, take where this was headed and just enjoy herself? Enjoy *him*?

When Cooper's mouth moved up to the valley between her breasts, his tongue dancing over her skin as his fingertips dipped inside the edge of her panties, Kelsey grabbed at his wrist.

"Cooper, please," she gasped, "wait."

He stilled.

"What—what are we doing?"

His punch of laughter was hot against her breast. "If you don't know, I must not be doing it right."

The sudden tightness in her throat made it impossible to speak. No, he was doing everything right. She gave him a gentle squeeze to tell him so.

He pulled from her touch to lay his hands on her upper thighs. His gaze was intent as he looked at her. "Is something wrong?"

Kelsey peered at him through her over-long bangs and nodded. Wait—no, she didn't want him to know that. She hastily shook her head.

His soft chuckle sent a stab of longing so deep inside, it landed in a part of her she'd never felt before. Deep down inside where she'd hidden all her foolish childhood dreams of finding the happily ever promised to every little girl who'd ever read a fairy tale.

Scared at what that longing meant, she was off his lap like a shot.

"You don't want this to happen," she said.

Cooper remained on the couch, stretching out one arm along the back. "All evidence to the contrary."

Her gaze flickered below his waist before she turned away, busy redoing her jeans. "I don't want... Neither of us needs or wants a complication in our lives right now."

"Complication?"

Kelsey turned back. "We just met. You just got back to town and your son is your number one priority right now—"

Cooper rose from the couch and walked to where she stood, his steps slow and deliberate until he stopped right in front of her. With a gentle touch he forced her to look at him. "I know what my priorities are."

A soft cry came through the baby monitor. Cooper swore and dropped his hand. When the next cry was louder, he held up a finger, gestured he would be just a minute and disappeared down the hall.

Kelsey went into the kitchen and picked up her sweatshirt from the floor. Slipping it on, she zippered it up and grabbed her wet T-shirt.

"I know what I want. And what I need."

She froze, then realized Cooper's voice came from the baby monitor. Unable to stop herself, she inched closer to where the handheld device sat on the end table.

"So Anthony, got any advice for your old man?" He continued talking. "It seems I've gotten myself into somewhat unfamiliar territory…."

Kelsey found herself drawn to the warmth and humor in Cooper's voice, even when a rustling noise and the sound of Anthony's babbling drowned out his words for a long moment before they became clear again.

"You think so? Yeah, that might just work."

What might work? What was he planning?

Oh, my, was he going to… Was Cooper Fortune planning on seducing her?

Kelsey's hand fisted, twisting her T-shirt into a

tight coil. Shaking her head, she backed away from the monitor.

No, she couldn't let that happen.

She'd been lured down that road too many times with promises of love, adventure and devotion, only to have it always end the same way. A dead end with her left behind to nurse a broken heart and a bruised spirit.

Squelching her rising panic, she turned on her heel and raced for the door.

Chapter Five

Cooper slipped past the sliding glass doors that led from the back patio to the kitchen of the main house at Molly's Pride. The smell of cinnamon was too tempting as a tray of freshly baked rolls, gooey icing melting into the curved tops, called out to him.

He put the baby carrier—with Anthony tucked inside happily sucking on his morning bottle—on the floor and reached for the closest roll.

"If you're looking for breakfast, you're too late."

Cooper froze, busted with his hands on the goods. He pulled one of the rolls free, turned around and grinned. "Sorry, I couldn't resist."

Evie, JR and Isabella's housekeeper, returned his smile. She placed a basket filled with freshly cut flowers on the counter and peeled off her gardening gloves. "I guess it's my own fault. Leaving those rolls out there in plain sight like that."

Cooper took a large bite. "Mmm, so good," he mumbled. "Thanks."

A moment later a tall glass of ice cold milk sat on the counter in front of him.

"Can't have one without the other," Evie said.

He preferred coffee but, having just taken another mouthful, Cooper only gave a "thumbs-up" sign in response. He polished off the last of the bun and downed the milk.

Wiping at his mouth with the napkin Evie provided, he watched as she sorted the colorful blossoms taken from the impressive gardens surrounding the hacienda. Cooper didn't recognize any of them by name, other than the famed Texas Bluebonnets and the long-stemmed yellow roses, but he knew just one would be the perfect way to put step two of his plan into action.

Step one—not calling to see if Kelsey was okay after she walked out on him yesterday.

Not that he had her phone number, but he did have Jessica's and a pretty good feeling that she'd share Kelsey's if he asked. But he'd kept busy by introducing Anthony to the fine art of baseball by watching a doubleheader and punching out an unending number of pushups.

"Can I ask one more favor?" he inquired.

"Have I done a single favor for you yet today?" Evie asked.

Cooper leaned against the counter. "You let me eat that world-class, awe-inspiring culinary confection."

"Flattery wins every time." The older woman turned to him. "What do you need?"

"Can I steal one of those roses?"

She smiled. "Got a special lady in mind for it?"

Oh, yeah. Very special.

Five minutes later, he walked across the patio again. The yellow rose in one hand, complete with a blue-checked bow thanks to Evie, and Anthony's baby carrier in the other. He headed for the horse barn. It was after nine in the morning and most of the ranch's cowboys were already well into their workday, and he knew Kelsey was, too. An hour ago he'd watched from his front porch as she and JR departed in one of the ranch trucks, a horse trailer attached.

"Okay, little guy, let's see if we can get this done covertly," Cooper said, slipping into the barn. He walked to Kelsey's office, set the rose on the center of her desk and wrote her a quick note.

Hope you have a good day! C.

A different message than the one she'd left him.

He'd returned yesterday afternoon after getting Anthony settled again to find the living room empty and a scribbled note left behind, held in place by a bottle of baby lotion.

I have to go. I'm sorry. K.

In retrospect, he shouldn't have been surprised to find her gone. He'd seen panic in her eyes when she'd bolted off his lap. At first, he'd thought he had done something to put that emotion there, but just like in the grocery store aisle, he'd also seen hunger and heat in those dark depths.

No, her fear had come from somewhere deep inside. Someone had hurt her—badly. And even though the fault wasn't his, all he wanted was the chance to make it up to her.

Cooper shook off his thoughts and grabbed Anthony's carrier. After a quick visit to Solo with fresh carrots and a promise of another ride soon, they left the barn and walked into the bright Texas sunshine. He snapped the baby's carrier into the buckled frame in the backseat of his truck and headed for town.

Forty-five minutes later, he was on the road again, minus his son. Kirsten had called this morning to ask how he and Anthony were doing. Cooper had been surprised she managed to hold off six full days before checking up on him, so he'd asked if she was free to keep an eye on Anthony for a few hours while he ran some errands. Her breathless yes told him just how much she missed the boy.

Then a quick call to Lily at the Double Crown Ranch to see if today was a good time for a visit with his Uncle William, and his morning plans were set.

Cooper smiled, remembering Kirsten's shock at the fully stocked diaper bag he'd left with her and his recommendation that peaches and applesauce went down much easier than peas when lunchtime came around. He just hoped Anthony wouldn't end up being confused by the time spent with her.

Turning onto the highway that would take him out to the Double Crown Ranch, he found himself wondering what his uncle's reaction would be to seeing him again. They weren't that close, their paths only crossing when William and his family had visited Red Rock during the summers Cooper had been dumped at the Fortune family ranch by his mother. Cooper had always envied the togetherness and easy warmth he'd witnessed between William and his kids.

Arriving at the ranch, he parked his truck and walked through the inner courtyard of the main house. The large, antique wooden door opened before he made it all the way up the stone steps.

"Cooper!"

Lily greeted him with a warm hug. Still a beautiful woman in her mid-sixties, she looked at home in her jeans and casual shirt.

Cooper returned her hug before closing the door behind him. "Hi, Lily. How are things going?"

"It's a good day," she said with a smile, leading him through the massive living room and into the kitchen. "But before we see William, I wanted to give you this."

She picked up a large, padded envelope from the countertop and handed it to him. Cooper looked at his name written in simple block lettering addressed to the Double Crown Ranch. "Where did this come from?"

"It was delivered this morning."

He read the return address, his heart giving a quick lurch as he recognized it as the bar where Lulu worked in Minnesota.

What the hell?

"Do you want to take a few minutes to see what's inside?" Lily asked. "The study is available if you'd like some privacy."

As much as he hated to do it, Cooper laid the package down. "No, thanks. I'll open it later."

"I know you're still feeling your way when it comes to being a father, but I do hope you'll bring Anthony out to the ranch for a visit soon." Lily opened the refrigerator and took out a glass pitcher. "We are so proud to welcome another Fortune into the family."

A flicker of pride filled Cooper's chest. "Thanks, Lily."

"You know, it's hard to believe it was because of your medallions that you all were able to figure out that sweet baby boy was a Fortune." Always the hostess, she spoke while putting together a tray of two empty glasses and a plate of cookies. "Thank goodness whoever had the baby left that medallion with him."

Cooper nodded, his fingers rubbing against his jeans where the coin now rested in his pocket. A Christmas gift from his mother decades ago, the medallion was a cheap knockoff. As artificial as the story Cindy had told him and his siblings about a buried treasure found outside of Red Rock by a Fortune ancestor. But now, he considered it his lucky charm and he carried it with him always.

Lily lifted the tray, waving off Cooper's attempt to carry it for her and headed for the other side of the kitchen. "William is enjoying the sunshine in the sitting area near the courtyard."

Cooper followed her, then hesitated when he saw his uncle in a chair near the double glass doors, staring out at the gardens. His brother and cousin had warned him that William had changed physically as well as emotionally during his ordeal, but Cooper was still surprised to see how the man, who'd always been tall, both in stature and in his larger-than-life presence, looked so still and detached in the oversize leather chair.

"William, darling, you have a visitor." Lily spoke to her fiancé. "Your nephew, Cooper, is here."

His uncle turned to look at him, no recognition in his eyes. "Hello."

"Hey, Uncle."

Silence filled the room for a moment before Lily set the tray on a rustic wood-and-wrought-iron coffee table. "I brought you a fresh pot of iced tea and some cookies."

"I'd rather have a beer," William said.

"No alcohol, dear. Doctor's orders. Besides, you have a physical therapy appointment this afternoon."

Cooper read frustration on his uncle's face as he sat on the leather couch opposite him, his gaze catching on the photo albums scattered across the end of the coffee table.

"Hang the doctors," William grumbled. "One beer isn't going to kill me."

"But I might if you continue to be a bear," Lily chided in a gentle tone as she leaned over and placed a kiss on William's silver-toned hair. "So, please behave yourself."

His uncle pulled away from Lily's touch, but she just gave his shoulder a squeeze before stepping back.

"I've got work to do in the other room," she said. "I'll leave you two to visit."

Cooper wanted to call out for her to stay, but instead he busied himself by pouring a glass of tea. He looked up to offer to do the same for his uncle in time to catch the older man's gaze as it followed Lily from the room.

"She's a good woman," he said, his voice low. "She takes care of me."

The words were said without any feelings or emotion behind them. Cooper had been told about his uncle's state of mind, but seeing him in person was unsettling. How was he supposed to respond to something like that? He'd never thought to ask Lily if there were any—geez, guidelines for lack of a better word—when it came to talking to William.

Cooper filled the second glass and held it out to his uncle, deciding to go with his gut, preferring honesty to anything else. "Yes, she loves you very much."

He took the glass. "So everyone keeps telling me. And you're Cooper Fortune, one of my sister Cindy's kids."

"Yes, one of the more unfortunate Fortunes."

"Don't say that." William's voice held a steely strength that wasn't there moments before as he sat up a little straighter in his chair. "I may not remember a damn thing about my life, but from what I've been told and seen in those photo albums, the Fortunes are a strong, proud family. All of them."

"All of us, you mean?"

The man slumped back against the cushion, the brief show of sentiment gone. "Is that why you're here? To give me another history lesson?"

Cooper took a long draw on his glass of tea before he spoke. He guessed it must be tiring being told stories of places, events and people that you couldn't remember. "I just wanted to stop by and say welcome home."

"You live in Red Rock?"

"I just moved here a few weeks ago. Before that I lived anywhere my horse and I ended up."

"A wandering cowboy, huh?" William's eyes trailed over him from his head to his boots. "You've got the look of a nomad."

Was that good or bad? "Not anymore. I'm putting down roots now."

Surprise filled Cooper at how easily he said those words. He'd never wanted to stay in one place before, the call of the open road had always been too strong to resist. But things were going good in Red Rock. Taking care of Anthony, being close to Ross and Frannie again, getting to know his cousins…

And Kelsey.

"You got someone special holding you to this place?" William rose from his chair to stand at the glass doors, looking outside.

Cooper stood, too, noticing the unsteadiness of the older man. "A couple of someones."

William nodded, but didn't say anything for a long moment until he finished off his drink. "How about some fresh air?"

He didn't know what the rules were, but he figured if the man wanted to go outside, he should be able to. Cooper followed his uncle onto the patio. "Sounds good to me."

"So, tell me about your adventures," William said. "Where have you been over the years?"

Cooper spoke as they walked through the gardens, circled back to the patio and sat at an outdoor table shaded by a large canvas umbrella. His uncle didn't ask many questions, but seemed interested in Cooper's stories and Cooper was surprised to check his watch and see ninety minutes had gone by.

"Well, I hate to end this visit, but I need to be heading out." Cooper rose from his chair, digging into his pocket for his keys. "It was good to see you, Uncle William."

"It was nice to meet—to see you again, too, Cooper."

A clanging noise had Cooper glancing at the table. The medallion he'd talked to Lily about had come out of his pocket when he'd pulled out his keys. He reached for it, but his uncle beat him to it.

"What was that—?" The man's fingers tightened on the coin. "Where did you get this?"

Surprised at the hard tone in his uncle's voice, Cooper held back from reaching for the medallion. "I've had it for years. It was a gift from my mother."

Remaining silent, he watched as his uncle studied the coin intently, turning it over and over in his hand. When Lily came through the door, he motioned to her to remain quiet, gesturing toward William. A look of concern came over her features as she joined him.

"This is mine." William's tone held an air of certainty. "This belongs to me."

A quick glance at Lily told Cooper she was as taken aback as him by his uncle's claim. "Actually, I got that when I was a kid for Christmas one year. It's just a worthless fake, but my brothers and sister each got one. We've all managed to hold onto them over the years, so I guess they mean something after all."

William shook his head. "No, this is mine."

"Darling, Cooper just told you that belongs to—"

Cooper laid a hand on her arm, stopping her. He didn't have any idea what was going on, but his uncle's insistence was the first real emotion he'd witnessed from the man since he arrived. "That's okay. If he wants to keep it, he can."

Gratitude crossed Lily's features. "Thank you."

"I've got to be heading out."

"I'll walk you to the door." Lily turned to William. "Cooper's leaving now and I'm going to show him out. I'll be right back."

His uncle nodded, his fingers closing into a fist around the coin as he stared off into the distance. They left him and walked back inside. Lily handed Cooper his envelope as they headed for the front door.

He'd forgotten about the package, but now Cooper was filled with a sudden need to see what was inside. Leaning down, he gave Lily a kiss on the cheek.

"Thank you so much for coming," she said. "I don't know what's gotten into William over that medallion of yours, but it means so much to me that you are letting him hold onto it. It's the first thing that's triggered such a powerful show of emotion in him since he's been back. I'm taking that as a good sign."

Lily opened the door for him. "And I'll make sure nothing happens to it."

He believed her, surprised at how important the coin had become to him in such a short amount of time. "Thanks."

Cooper headed back to his truck. Once inside, he started it up and headed off the ranch, but pulled over on the side of the road before he hit the highway. Ripping open the package, he turned it upside down. Out fell a letter, a couple of envelopes and a small jewelry box.

Unfolding the letter, Cooper read the words written by the owner of the bar where Lulu had worked. He stated the enclosed paperwork had been left behind in her employee folder when she quit her job last December. It had been misfiled, which is why it was found only recently.

The owner had known she'd left town, as she'd sold the contents of the jewelry box to him to have enough cash for the trip. Since learning of her death, her former boss felt it only right that the items went to Lulu's son. The only address left behind had been under Cooper's name in Red Rock, Texas, so the man hoped Cooper could make sure the baby got these things.

Stunned, Cooper looked at the envelopes and found one sealed with the words "my son" written across the front. The other one was open, and he pulled out an official document with "Birth Certificate" written in bold font across the top.

Blood pounded at his temples as he quickly scanned the document, searching for his name. There it was, right where it should be, listing him as the baby's father. Elation filled him as he read the details surrounding his son's birth. The date, time and his weight and size the moment he came into this world.

He should've been there.

He should've been there to help Lulu through the labor, to cut the umbilical cord, to hold his son in his hands as he took his first breaths.

The stinging in his eyes made it hard to read. He blinked away the pain as the words that made up Anthony's full name came into focus.

His real name.

"What happened to you? You look like you've seen a ghost."

Cooper ignored his brother, Ross, as he slid into the booth at Red, still listening to the woman on the other end of the phone. He'd called Kirsten on his way to the restaurant, asked if she minded keeping Anthony for a bit longer, which of course she didn't.

"Jeremy came home for lunch and we just finished eating. I was about to give Anthony a bottle and put him down for a nap. Is that all right?"

"That's fine and thanks," Cooper replied. "I'm at Red

with my brother—" he paused when his sister, Frannie, slid into the booth next to Ross "—and my sister. I should be by in about an hour to get him."

"Take your time. I've loved being with him again."

Cooper ended the call as a waiter came by, dropping off menus and taking their drink order. He waited until they were alone before he laid the envelope from Minnesota on the table.

"I found out Anthony's real name. William Antonio Carlton Fortune."

That statement got both Ross and Frannie's attention.

Cooper emptied the padded envelope on the table and explained about his visit with Lily and William, the package being delivered there and what he found when he opened it.

"Wow, that's unbelievable," Ross said as he examined the baby's birth certificate. "At least you're officially listed as the kid's father and he has the Fortune name. I'm guessing you aren't planning to start calling him William?"

The waiter appeared again with their drinks and they quickly ordered their meals. Cooper waited until they were alone again before he spoke.

"No, Anthony knows his name. I have no idea why Lulu called him that instead of Will or William or Billy, but I'm guessing the Antonio in his name is because I once told her San Antonio is my birth place."

Frannie picked up the sealed envelope. "I'm guessing you aren't planning to open this?"

Cooper took a moment, downing a large swallow from his glass of ice water. Curiosity and the still-unknown conditions surrounding Lulu and Anthony's arrival in

Red Rock had him wanting to see what was inside, but his sense of honor to the envelope being sealed held him off.

"I haven't decided yet," he said honestly, "but it's not something I need to worry about right now."

His sister stroked the jewelry box. "Have you opened this?"

He shook his head.

"May I?"

He nodded. Inside they found a pin with a woman's portrait on it and a pearl necklace. Cooper had never seen either piece before. He could only guess they had once belonged to someone in Lulu's family.

"Oh, they're beautiful," Frannie said. "The base of this cameo pin looks like it could be black onyx. Anthony's mother must've wanted them to go to him someday."

Deciding to keep the fact that Lulu needed to sell the jewelry to pay for her way to Texas to himself, Cooper closed the box and put it and the letters back in the envelope.

Ross returned the birth certificate. "So, how did things go with Uncle William? Julie and I were out there last week to see him, but he was still very distant."

"It went okay, I guess. I thought I was prepared to see him, but except for one moment, he's very different from the William Fortune we all know."

"What moment was that?" Frannie asked.

Cooper explained about their uncle's reaction to seeing his medallion. "He wanted it so desperately I let him keep it. But you guys know we've always thought those coins were pieces of junk that Cindy picked up in Vegas on her way home for Christmas."

"And that silly story she told us about buried pirate treasure brought to Red Rock from South Padre Island," Frannie added. "Of course, at the time, I believed her."

They stopped talking as the waiter arrived with their food.

"You were young," Ross said, after taking a bite. "Of course you believed her. We all wanted to believe the stories she told us. It just got harder as the years went by."

"We were always going to have a big house with a huge yard, remember?" Cooper dug into his chicken enchiladas. "With a swimming pool and a barn and one of those wooden playground sets with a swing for each of us? Boy, no one could spin a tale like Cindy Fortune."

"And then another 'man of her dreams' would come along and we'd be left in the dust." Frannie spoke with a soft voice. "Sometimes I'm still amazed I have a stable and loving marriage after watching all the relationships our mother went through."

"With everything you've gone through, again thanks to Mom, you've earned your happily-ever-after with Roberto," Ross said.

"Yes, I did, and I'm glad to see at least one of my brothers has joined me in the world of being joyfully married." She nudged him in the ribs. "Even if it did take you forever to get there."

Ross returned her smile. "Julie was well worth waiting for. Now we just need to get this one," he nodded to Cooper, "and Flint, to join us."

Frannie laughed. "I'm not sure there's a member of my fair sex who can put up with either one of them."

"You do realize I can hear you?" Cooper waved his fork in the air. "Seeing how I'm sitting right here?"

"Yeah, and amazingly you haven't been scared off." Ross grinned as he picked up his glass of iced tea. "Of course, we haven't actually used the words 'settle' and 'down' in the same sentence yet."

"Maybe I'm looking at things a little differently now."

His sister's eyes narrowed. "What things?"

"You know, the future, putting down roots, settling down." Cooper paused to clear his throat, then he continued. "And I think I might've found the one worth waiting for."

Chapter Six

Cooper's brother and sister stared at him for a full minute before they turned to look at each other, and then back at him, clearly shocked.

Well, he was, too. He had no freaking clue where that declaration had come from. When Ross spouted off about Julie being the right woman for him, the words just burst from his mouth. "Forget I said that. I must be sniffing too much diaper cream lately."

"Is it Anthony?" Ross asked. "You seem to have taken to fatherhood pretty well, Coop. You don't need to find a mother for him right away."

Cooper pushed back against the booth's seat and sat a bit straighter. "I'm not looking for a mother for my son."

"Why not?" Frannie asked. "If you're crazy enough to be thinking about settling down already, you can't go off and marry some floozy who thinks you've got access to a lot of money because of your last name."

"Well, she'd be wrong about that. My bank account was earned the hard way. And Kelsey's not a floozy."

"Who's Kelsey?" Ross and Frannie asked in unison.

Damn. He'd managed to shove his size-ten boot right into his big, fat mouth. "Kelsey Hunt. She works for JR on his ranch. She's in charge of his equine program."

"I don't think I've met her, but I've heard JR talk about how great she is with his horses." Ross reached for his drink. "It figures you'd find someone who shares your affinity for the four-legged creatures."

"I haven't found anyone," Cooper protested, backpedaling. "I only met her a few days ago."

Less than a week, he realized. Why did it seem like he'd known her longer than that?

Maybe because he found her so easy to talk to? Or the way she'd pitched in and helped with the baby? Not to mention how right it felt to hold her in his arms and how fast his blood boiled when she touched him. But did that really mean he was ready to settle down? Maybe leaving that rose on her desk this morning hadn't been such a good idea after all.

"Well, considering you have more than your fair share of notches on your—"

"Watch it," Cooper interrupted, Ross's words pulling him from his thoughts. "We're in mixed company here."

"Yeah, the same 'company' that knows you started your dating career before you turned fifteen," Frannie snorted. "And you haven't slowed since. Don't you think it's a bit soon to be thinking this Kelsey is 'the one'?"

Cooper didn't know what pissed him off more, his sister's tone or the way she emphasized the end of her question. "I think I'm smart enough, and experienced enough, to know the right thing when I see it."

"Have you ever felt this way about any other woman?" Frannie continued.

He hadn't. Not once, and he'd been dating for a quarter of a century. All types, from secretaries to showgirls, and he'd never considered the idea of asking any of them to share his last name. Hell, he was usually out the door with their not-so-subtle hints to stick around still ringing in his ears despite him being up front with them from the very beginning that he wasn't a relationship kind of guy.

"Did you feel this way about Anthony's mother?"

Ouch, direct hit. Cooper's grip tightened on the napkin next to his plate of food. "No, I didn't."

Contrition filled Frannie's eyes. She laid a hand over his. "Coop, I'm sorry. I didn't mean that the way it sounded."

"You could've fooled me," Ross muttered under his breath.

Frannie shot him a dark look before concentrating on Cooper again. "It's just that I know how easy it is to want to believe someone is perfect for you only to find out too late that you were wrong."

"You're talking about your history, sis. Before Roberto, that is."

"And our mother's history," Frannie countered. "We grew up with more 'uncles' and pretend daddies than we can remember. She never presented a good example for any of us to follow of what it takes to have a strong and loving relationship. I just don't want you to get in over your head."

"Who, me?"

"I know you, big brother." Frannie smiled.

"Hell, that doesn't mean Cooper can't ask Kelsey for a date, right?" Ross said. "I mean, you're not at the bended-knee stage yet, are you?"

Cooper had no idea what stage he was in.

For someone brand-new in his life, Kelsey was so familiar to him—yet having her in his arms was like nothing he'd ever felt before. It was almost as if he'd been biding his time with a life lived on the road—no ties, no settling down—until he met her.

"Cooper?"

He blinked and saw amusement in his brother's gaze while Frannie's blue eyes carried a hint of concern.

"Hey, don't lose sleep over this," he replied. "I'm far from shopping for a ring."

"See?" Ross leaned over and nudged at Frannie's shoulder. "Stop your worrying, mother hen. There's nothing wrong with him spending some time with a pretty lady at this weekend's Spring Fling."

"That's this weekend?" Cooper asked. The annual fair was a big draw for Red Rock and it'd been years since Cooper had attended.

Ross nodded. "Lots of food, rides, a midway filled with game booths, crafts and dancing."

"Sounds like the place to be."

"And Anthony will be a perfect chaperone," Frannie added. "How much trouble can you get in with a five-month-old around?"

Friday night and nowhere to go.

Not that Kelsey cared. It'd been a long day with her two newest rescue horses, using an approach and retreat method as she worked to get them comfortable with her being near their faces. Both horses had been victims of abuse that left the animals head shy, but they were coming along, slowly but surely.

And at almost eight o'clock, Kelsey was already in her favorite, ages-old, two-sizes-too-big, cotton pajamas with a classic Doris Day romantic comedy ready to go. She'd just covered her face in the latest organic facial cream guaranteed to give her baby-smooth skin even if it did feel like a cross between pancake batter and whipped cream. With her hair wrapped in a towel to allow a conditioning treatment to soak into her long tresses, all she needed was a glass of wine to complete her evening.

But her sister, who was in charge of bringing tonight's refreshments, was running late.

Moving the mixing bowls containing two other facial options to one side of her kitchen table, her arm brushed against the single yellow rose in the bud vase. She smiled, remembering how she'd returned to her office yesterday afternoon to find Cooper's sweet gift on her desk.

She'd expected him to come by, maybe to ask why she'd walked out on him. He never showed, even after she'd stayed late in her office tackling never-ending paperwork. Kelsey had looked out the window that faced Cooper's cottage more times than she cared to count. Despite seeing him twice today, both times at a distance, she hadn't found the courage to go up and talk to him.

What could she say?

That she was all about being wild and free except when a five-month-old baby was in the picture? That she'd been burned too many times in the past to take a chance?

Maybe she was overthinking all of this. It was just a few kisses. Perhaps the rose was just Cooper being sweet and—oh, could he have meant it as an apology?

When the ding from the oven timer went off, Kelsey jumped. She shook her head to rid it of any thoughts related to the sexy cowboy living just a few hundred yards away and reached for an oven mitt. Removing the warm and gooey Mexican cheese dip from the oven, she placed it, along with a bowl of nacho chips, on the coffee table in front of the couch. Adding two wineglasses, she reached for a chip as a knock came to her door.

"Well, it's about time you got here," she called out, walking across the open space that made up the combined living room and kitchen of her apartment. She yanked the door open. "I've already glooped on the strawberry facial stuff, so you'll have either blueberry or…"

Her voice faded when two sets of matching brown eyes stared back at her. The first pair was wide-eyed and filled with sweetness and innocence. The other hooded, but not enough to hide the smoldering sexiness that seemed to live there permanently.

"Cooper." His name fell from her lips.

A slow grin crossed the man's face as he shifted his son from one shoulder to the other. "You know, with the way you say my name, it's a good thing my hands are full at the moment."

Or you'd be in my arms again.

The words were unspoken, but Kelsey heard them in her head as clearly as if he'd said them aloud. Her blood hummed in her veins as the memory of his hands on her, and her hands on him, caused every inch of her body to respond.

"Of course," he continued in a low, sexy drawl, "I'd be hoping that pink concoction on your face was edible."

"Oh!"

Kelsey's hands flew to her cheeks, her fingertips sinking into the strawberry-flavored cream.

"Oh, no!"

She pulled her hands away and wiped them on her pajama top, her actions pulling the deep V of her neckline even lower. Realizing the thinness of her pajamas and the fact her bra was currently lying on the floor of her bedroom, she whirled away from the doorway and raced into the kitchen, reaching for the closest dish towel.

"Can we come in?" Cooper asked. "You're letting out all the cool air."

The air-conditioning unit in the far window agreed with him and kicked on with a not-so-quiet hum. Kelsey gave a quick jerk of her head as she concentrated on wiping her hands. She then aimed for her face when a gentle hand grabbed her wrist.

"Don't do that." Cooper stood inches away from her. His eyes scanned the room, taking in the food waiting on the coffee table and the beauty products littering her kitchen table before they returned to her. "Not on our account. We've obviously intruded on a special evening."

"It's beauty night for the Hunt sisters. Pedicures and facials...this is all organic," Kelsey babbled as she waved at her face. "We do it once a month or so. Our folks watch Jess's kids. I—ah, I thought you were her. Jessica."

"I get that a lot." He released his hold on her, but didn't step away. "Must be the baby in my arms."

Kelsey smiled and dropped her hands, but then Cooper's dark brown eyes deepened when his gaze again traveled the length of her body all the way to her bare toes. The heat in his eyes seemed to torch every exposed inch of her skin.

She clutched the towel to her chest. "What are you doing here?"

He shifted the baby to a basket hold, low in front of his midsection, one hand across Anthony's chest while the other cradled his bottom. The movement caused his blue T-shirt to tighten across the width of his chest as the sinewy muscles of his arms bunched at the short sleeves hugging his biceps. "Well, we were wondering if you have any plans for tomorrow night."

Kelsey forced her gaze from those amazing arms and the memory of how it felt to be held by them to concentrate on Cooper's face. "Plans?"

He cleared his throat and held his son away from his body, probably to avoid Anthony's kicking feet. "Yeah, it's been years since I've been to the Spring Fling and this will be Anthony's first. We thought you might like to join us."

A date.

Cooper Fortune was asking her out on a date.

Not just him, but him and Anthony. Would it technically be a date? It'd be the three of them, not much different than when she tagged along with her sister to help with her kids. So it wasn't a date. They'd just be hanging out together and the Spring Fling always included a crowd, and trying to maneuver a stroller while eating or perusing the crafts area would be difficult for someone alone—

"Kelsey?"

"Yes?"

"Is that a 'yes' you'll go or a 'yes' you need me to repeat the question?"

"Ah, yeah—I mean, yes, I'll go to the Spring Fling with you. I'm sure this little guy will be a handful, and you'll need all the help you can get."

"Okay." A perplexed expression crossed Cooper's features. "I'll be by to pick you up after Anthony gets up from his nap and I get him fed. Say around six?"

"Sounds good."

"Well, I better get out of here. Say goodbye to the pretty lady, Anthony."

Kelsey laughed when the baby seemed to follow his father's instructions and waved. She grabbed his tiny hand and gave it a quick shake, then walked them back to the door.

Cooper stepped out onto the small covered landing. He turned to face her again, placing his son back to his shoulder. He then leaned in and gave her a quick kiss on the mouth.

Stunned, Kelsey watched as he wiped away the gummy remnants of her facial from his chin stubble.

He licked his lips and grinned. "Hmm, not bad. But you taste sweeter. See you tomorrow."

He loped down the long stairs that led to the grassy area below. Kelsey watched him go, then shut the door, unable to move except to lean back, her towel-covered head hitting the door with a thump.

Why had he done that? Why had he kissed her?

In a few short sentences she'd convinced—no, fooled

was a better word—herself into thinking tomorrow night didn't mean anything.

Did it mean something?

No. She couldn't let it. A knock on the door had her swinging around. It had to be Cooper, back to explain and apologize—

"Cooper, I don't think—"

The sight of her sister stopped her words.

"I'm guessing you were expecting someone else?"

"Hey, Jess."

"Wow, you look…I don't know, happy and scared to death at the same time, if that's possible." Her sister gently swayed the wine bottle cradled in her hand. "Should I have brought two of these?"

Kelsey took the wine and waved her inside. "Sorry, I thought maybe Cooper had returned."

"Meaning he was already here once tonight?"

Kelsey nodded as she headed for the coffee table and grabbed the corkscrew she'd left there. Working on the bottle she effectively ignored her sister's pointed gaze.

"And you looked like that?"

Still ignoring her sister and how her hands shook as she poured the wine into the two glasses, Kelsey then took one glass for herself and handed one to Jessica.

"What did he want?"

"He asked me to go with him and Anthony to the Spring Fling tomorrow."

Jessica took her glass. "Hey, that's great—"

"No, it's not. This has disaster written all over it. It's one thing to be neighborly, help him with the baby when it comes to picking out food. But a date? On top of kissing him? That's taking things way too—"

"Whoa, wait a minute." Her sister cut her off. "You kissed him?"

"He kissed me. Then I kissed him back." Kelsey took a large gulp of wine. "We kissed each other."

"Just now?"

Kelsey shook her head. "Wednesday. After I helped him give Anthony a bath."

"How was it?"

"The bath?"

"The kissing."

"Oh, it was… He was…"

Her sister dropped to the couch and leaned back against the cushions with a sigh. "Oh, I remember what that was like."

"What?"

"The inability to put into words what a man does to you."

"I'm not… He's not…"

Jessica smiled as she ran a finger around the edge of her glass. "Boy, you've got it bad."

She did.

And for a man she'd known just over a week.

All the strength left her and she slowly sank to the couch next to her sister. "Jess, what am I going to do?"

"Hon, I know you're scared, but you need to let go of your past." Jessica patted her on the knee. "You remember what Mom always says about gauging a man's worth?"

Kelsey nodded. "How a man acts around children and animals will show his true character."

"And you've seen both firsthand with Cooper. You said yourself he's wonderful with his horse. As for the way he is with his son...well, his lack of experience is far outpaced by his obvious love and commitment."

Everything her sister said was true, but that didn't make the jump back into the world of dating any easier. Especially since her last two boyfriends had been great with animals, too. It was their inability to treat her decently that got in the way. "I'm going to screw this up, Jess. Just like always. I'm going to fall too hard, too fast and then—"

"So, just take it slow this time," her sister said. "It's only a date, right? He didn't get down on one knee, did he?"

"I've only known the guy a week!"

"I fell in love with Pete when I was barely a teenager," Jessica reminded her. "There aren't any rules when it comes to finding your true love."

"This isn't true love." Kelsey stood and marched to the kitchen table. Placing her wineglass down with a thunk, she grabbed the bowl of blueberry facial. "It's just...hormones."

"Okay, whatever you say." Jess joined her as she pulled hair into a tight ponytail. "I'm guessing you're whipping that fruity mixture into submission for my benefit?"

Kelsey stopped her frenzied churning and scooped up a handful of the facial. "Yes, and close your mouth. My aim isn't so good."

Jessica complied, but the sparkling laughter in her eyes told Kelsey how hard it was for her sister to comply. She smoothed on the creamy blend leaving only her sister's eyes and mouth uncovered.

"Okay, go ahead." Kelsey went to the sink and washed her hands. "I know you're dying to ask something."

"What are you going to wear?"

"Jeans and a T-shirt," she replied, knowing her sister was asking about tomorrow's date. "What else?"

"Oh, come on. The man's only seen you in jeans and T-shirts since you met him."

"Don't forget this lovely outfit." Kelsey turned around, hands held aloft as if she was a model posing for a photo shoot. "Complete with a ratty towel turban and my face covered in strawberry gunk."

Jessica laughed and grabbed a bottle of nail polish as she toed off her flip-flops. "Don't you have anything in your closet that's flirty and sexy and guaranteed to knock his boots off?"

Kelsey steadied the towel on her head as she looked down at her pajamas. She cringed at the image of her Cooper had left here with, but flirty and sexy?

"Wait, I know what you should wear!" Her sister jumped up from her chair and headed for Kelsey's bedroom.

From the noise, Kelsey knew Jess was rummaging in her closet, but she doubted her sister would find anything. Her whole world was working with horses and being in a barn all day.

What could she possibly have that would give the prescribed effect her sister suggested? Did she want to knock Cooper's boots off—figuratively or otherwise? And what would she do if she managed to accomplish just that?

"You can wear this," Jessica said, returning with a dress dangling from her fingertips. "It's soft and feminine and sexy—"

"That? I haven't worn that since Mom and Dad's anniversary party five years ago." Kelsey stared at her sister. "And you spent most of that night telling me it was too short!"

"Like I said," Jessica said with a grin. "It's perfect!"

Chapter Seven

Cooper stepped down from his truck, his boots so shiny he could see his freshly shaved reflection in them. He tucked his starched shirt back down into the waistband of his jeans and straightened the rodeo buckle he'd won six months before he'd been legally old enough to drink.

Eyeing his Stetson in the backseat, he decided to leave it there since he'd just take it off again on the drive to the fairgrounds. He looked to the other side of the seat where Anthony sat, smiling and drooling, safely locked into his car seat.

He wondered if he should leave him there. The stairs to Kelsey's apartment were only a few feet away. He'd be able to get to her front door and never take his eyes off the truck.

Better not, he decided, as he rounded the freshly

washed vehicle's front end, reaching for the back door on his son's side of the truck.

"Please, don't worry about moving him. I'm ready to go."

He turned at the sound of Kelsey's voice.

The air disappeared from his lungs before he could brace for the effect. Damn. He managed to lock his knees and stay upright, a major victory, when he caught sight of his date.

He thought he'd gotten used to the now-familiar kick to the gut every time he saw this lady. A kick that even happened last night when the only things he could see in all that creamy goo were her beautiful eyes and luscious mouth.

Not this time.

Nope, this felt like he'd been knocked on his butt by a rearing bronco. He half expected to look up and see a ring of dancing stars circling over his head.

What he saw instead was Kelsey, standing outside her apartment on the postage-stamp-size landing. Her hair flowed over her shoulders in a dark shiny curtain, and he realized it was the first time he'd seen her wearing it down. Lightly tanned skin was laid bare thanks to the sleeveless, peach-colored sundress that hit her midthigh. Sexy sandals revealed the results of last night's beauty regimen with polished toes that matched her dress.

She held tight to the stairs' handrail while her smile, a mixture of anxious and sweet, dimmed. "Cooper? Is everything all right?"

Everything was perfect.

She was perfect.

He blinked hard and resisted the urge to make sure

his hair wasn't a mess. He should've cut it today, but opted for cleaning out the truck instead.

After a quick glance at Anthony, he forced his legs to move to the bottom of the stairs. "Yeah…everything's…"

His voice trailed off as she started toward him, bringing those lean, toned legs closer and closer. The image flashed in his head of him kissing one delicate ankle before moving upward until he reached the smooth, sweet—

"Cooper?"

He broke free of his fantasy and realized she'd stopped on the second to last step. They now stood eye to eye.

"You can close your mouth." Kelsey's fingers lightly tapped beneath his chin. "And thank you."

He grinned, enjoying that she knew she'd taken his breath away. "You're welcome."

"You clean up nice, too."

The tip of her tongue swiped across her lips. A wet shine remained that Cooper wanted to devour, along with the rest of her. He fought off the impulse, reminding himself again, that this was just a friendly date, a night on the town.

With a woman who had the ability to drop him to his knees.

Literally and with pleasure.

He gestured at the truck. "Ah, you ready to go?"

"Sure."

Kelsey stepped down the last two steps and walked to the passenger side. He opened the door, noticing her quick study of the amount of space between the ground and the seat. She hesitated for a moment before grabbing the hold bar and hoisting herself inside.

Suddenly grateful for the oversize tires that raised the truck's chassis almost two feet off the ground, he enjoyed the sight of her dress inching even higher on those gorgeous legs. He then realized he'd missed out on the chance to get his hands on her in the guise of offering her assistance.

That was probably a good thing.

He shut the door and headed for the driver's side, taking the long way around the end of the truck. He used the extra steps to remind himself again why he'd waited until the last minute to make plans with Kelsey.

Talking with Ross and Frannie had him second-guessing his choices, and he hated it. He'd always followed his gut when it came to deciding everything from what job to take next, to when to walk away or stick around for the fight.

So, he'd ignored the almost magnetic pull this lady seemed to have over him and steered clear of her for nearly forty-eight hours. Then he'd decided to follow his own personal code, which coincided with his brother's advice, and ask her for a date.

"The vehicle only moves when you do."

Cooper jerked, heat crossing his face. He'd gotten behind the wheel and put on his seat belt, but the truck was still in park with the engine running, the radio turned to a local country music station.

"Right." His fingers moved to the button that controlled the blast of the air-conditioning. "You mind if I turn this up?"

He looked over and watched Kelsey turn back from

where she'd cooed a soft hello to Anthony before grabbing her seatbelt and clicking it into place.

An unsettled feeling hit him in the chest.

She'd taken a moment to talk to his son. What's the big deal in that? Refusing to scrutinize why it meant so much to him, he pushed the feeling aside, cranked the fan to high, letting loose a blast of cold air, and put the truck in reverse.

Glancing over his shoulder, his gaze landed on Anthony for a moment before it slid over the lady next to him, her long hair blowing off her shoulders in the artificial breeze. The same breeze lifted a light strawberry scent off her skin, filling the truck's cabin and his head.

He focused on his driving, but his gaze constantly moved to the mirrors to keep an eye on his son and to Kelsey, who seemed to have no problem keeping her gaze focused on the road. An awkward silence prevailed as they reached the crowded parking lot for the fairgrounds ten minutes later and found a spot.

Cooper turned off the engine and exited the truck. He reached Kelsey's door just as she'd opened it. This time he reached for her, placing his hands around her waist and easily lifted her to the ground.

"Oh, you don't have to do that—ohhh," Kelsey said. "That feels good."

A shiver raced through her and her soft exhale went right to his gut before taking a hard right southward, distracting him from realizing exactly what that sexy sound meant.

He moved his hands from her hips to her upper arms, feeling the raised goose bumps on her skin. "Are you cold? Damn, you're freezing. Why didn't you say anything?"

"You seemed to prefer the arctic temperature." She shivered again as he rubbed her arms. Unclenching her fingers, she placed her hands to his chest. "Mmm, that feels wonderful."

"You should've said something."

"I didn't think you were in the mood to talk."

He stilled, the angle of the early-evening sun making it hard to see her eyes. Her fingertips flexed against the stiff material of his shirt. He had to hold back his own groan as he pulled her closer. So close, he could feel her dress brush against the front of his jeans.

"Maybe we should just do it and get it over with," Kelsey whispered.

It'd been a while since Cooper had made love in the back of a pickup and it usually involved advanced planning that included privacy and soft blankets—and no children. Of course, that didn't stop the image of him and Kelsey, skin to skin, beneath a star-filled sky from flashing inside his head.

"Kiss me, Cooper."

Huh?

She tunneled her fingers into the hair that lay against his shirt collar and tugged his head down until their lips met. Her tongue moved over his mouth and he immediately allowed her entrance, meeting her more than halfway. The desire to crush her to his chest raced through him, but he held off and allowed the beautiful woman in his arms to control this moment.

Arching her back, she reached up and pressed her curves against him. He flattened his hands to her back to hold her in place and keep his fingers from inching southward to find out exactly what she wore beneath the silky material of her dress.

It wasn't until distant catcalls and whistles from other Spring Fling patrons reached his ears that Cooper pulled back, ending the connection between them.

"There..." Kelsey lowered herself from her tiptoes and withdrew her hands, busying herself with putting her purse back up on one shoulder. "Much better."

With great reluctance, Cooper let his hands fall from her back as he heaved a deep breath and slowly released it. "If you say so."

"Now we can enjoy our evening without wondering if the kissing that happened the other day was as good as we thought."

"You were wondering that?" he asked.

"Weren't you?"

He shook his head, unable to contain the grin tugging at one corner of his mouth. "No, ma'am."

"Oh."

"I never had any doubt how good it was," Cooper said, unable to stop himself from touching her, his thumb lightly brushing over the throbbing pulse point at the base of her neck. "But thanks for the reminder."

She swallowed, but didn't move from his touch. He liked that. "Speaking of reminders," he continued, "I think we should get Anthony out of his car seat before he realizes the truck's engine is off."

"Oh, my!" This time Kelsey did spring out of his reach. "I can't believe I forgot—that I kissed you instead of—"

"Hey, no harm done." Cooper opened the door to the backseat. "See, he's fine."

Anthony turned his head at the noise and offered a sloppy grin around a plastic teething ring.

"As long as he's got something in his mouth, he's a happy guy."

It took some effort, but Cooper managed to cut off any relation those words had to what his own mouth had just been doing. He reached for the diaper bag and stroller. It took a few minutes to figure out how to unfold the complex device, but between the two of them they got everything locked in place, including Anthony, who thankfully still had a dry diaper.

"Whew!" Grabbing his Stetson from the seat, Cooper placed it on his head. He took the diaper bag from Kelsey and shoved it into the open space in the back of the stroller. "I think we're all set. Ready to introduce this little guy to a Red Rock tradition?"

Kelsey nodded and walked between the parked vehicles toward the open area leading to the concessions. "Let's start with food. All this work has revved up my appetite."

He flexed his fingers, relaxing his grip on the stroller's handles as he pushed his son alongside her. "And here I thought I had something to do with that."

She tilted her head and looked at him with a smile. "Relax and enjoy ourselves, remember?"

"Oh, I remember, all right."

An hour later, Cooper was sure his head was going to explode thanks to the images bombarding him.

Watching Kelsey dive into her plate of Texas barbecue, licking the sauce from her fingers with ease, having no idea what the sight of her tongue wrapped around those long digits did to him. Her shifting close to him, pressing those curves against his arm as he moved the

baby's stroller through the crowd or whenever she introduced him to people who stopped to say hello. Enjoying
the way she happily played Anthony's favorite game of
"drop the toy, watch the grown-up pick it up" they had
going on.

And boy, did the girl love junk food.

After dinner there'd been a bag of cotton candy—
more finger-licking to wreak havoc on his libido—as
they walked through the craft area. She claimed it kept
her from spending money, but he'd seen her eyes light
up when she spotted a rust-colored blanket with purple,
white and turquoise accents in the booth that housed
Isabella Fortune's hand-woven creations.

He'd overheard the two ladies talking as he stood
nearby with JR, Isabella's husband, and saw Kelsey's
disappointment at the price. Slipping his cousin enough
cash to cover the purchase and his truck keys when
JR offered to stash the blanket there, Cooper promised to stop back on the way out to get his keys. He
wanted Kelsey to have something special to remember
tonight.

As they entered the Spring Fling midway minutes
later to test their gaming skills, she was finishing off
a cherry Popsicle that stained the inside of her mouth
a bright red and made him want to taste her all over
again.

"What's an aardvark's favorite pizza topping?"

Pulled from his thoughts by her question, Cooper
realized she was reading a riddle off the empty Popsicle
stick. "I don't know. What?"

"*Ant*-chovies."

Cooper groaned, but Kelsey laughed and a desperate

need to feel her mouth under his again raced through his veins.

She must've read the need on his face because she turned toward the closest booth, digging into her purse. "Come on, let's play this one. I'm feeling lucky!"

He was willing to show her just how lucky they both could be, but instead, Cooper eyed the milk bottles stacked three layers high on the other side of the booth. Often the bottles were made with leaded bottoms, making it near impossible to knock over the entire tower and win a prize, unless the thrower concentrated on the base of the first row.

Kelsey aimed right at the middle of the stack with each of her three tosses, succeeding in upending only the top two layers. After she finished, he handed over control of the baby's stroller and laid down his money. He quickly fired off three shots and ended up with a bright purple sorry-excuse-for-a-stuffed-animal for a prize.

"For me?" Kelsey's eyes widened as he held out the creature to her. "You don't want to keep it for Anthony?"

"Purple's not really his color."

The quick press of her lips to his cheek wasn't the kind of thank-you kiss he wanted, but Cooper would take it.

For now.

They moved on to a few more booths, taking turns so one of them was always keeping an eye on Anthony, whose bright eyes and gummy smile showed he was enjoying the evening as much as they were. Cooper didn't win any more prizes, mostly because he ended up playing against kids at the water-squirt and horse-racing games, so he purposely skewed his aim to allow for one of the young people to be the winner.

"That was very sweet of you." Kelsey hugged the dismal stuffed animal he'd won to her stomach as they watched a little girl walk away with a cartoon bear as big as she.

"Sweet? Forget it." Cooper tipped back the brim of his hat. "That munchkin's daddy has probably already taken her target practicing."

"You're a good man, Cooper Fortune."

Her words crawled deep inside him and joined that still-unstudied emotion from when he spotted her talking with Anthony in the truck. Both settled in his gut with a warmth he'd never felt before.

They neared the end of the midway and Cooper could see the strings of colored lights and paper lanterns that outlined the dance area through the trees. The sweet sound of live country music battled with the prerecorded classic rock blaring through speakers lining the gaming booths.

Kelsey paused and looked toward the dance floor before turning away. Cooper was filled with a sudden urge to get her into his arms as they moved to a twangy country classic accompanied by the slide of a steel guitar. Did she want the same thing? But what to do about Anthony? They couldn't leave him—

"Cooper, look!"

He turned and saw Kelsey had moved to stand before the basketball-throw booth. She'd already pulled the required five dollars for three shots from her purse by the time he reached her.

"Kels, don't waste your money." He grabbed her

hand, stopping her from handing over the cash. "This one is impossible to win."

"Maybe for you." She quirked one eyebrow at him as she flashed him a smile he felt all the way to his boot heels.

"For everyone."

"But it only takes one shot to win a prize."

Cooper angled Anthony's stroller to one side as a trio of teenage boys, tall and lanky, stepped up on the other side of Kelsey and laid down their money. "Here, watch these guys."

Each kid took his turn and eight throws in a row bounced off the backboard or missed the basket completely to end up on the cushioned area below.

Kelsey shoved her stuffed animal into Cooper's hands. She then turned to the boy who, down to his last shot, looked lost as to how to accomplish what his buddies hadn't.

A win.

"May I?" she asked, gesturing for the ball.

The teenager grinned and handed it to her. Cooper shoved down a flash of protectiveness at the kid's starry-eyed gaze and leaned in close to Kelsey's shoulder.

"The basketball is overinflated," he said in a low voice. "Never mind the fact the hoop is nowhere near regulation size. You need to do a shot called a tear drop. Arc it high and aim for nothing but net…."

Cooper's advice died as Kelsey released a perfect shot that never touched the metal rim, the ball making a neat swish through the net.

Then she did it again.

And again.

And again.

Fifteen dollars and ten perfect shots later, the kids cheered as the carnival worker handed over a stuffed pony that matched the average size of a newborn colt.

"For Anthony," she said, holding out the brown-and-black animal. "His first horse, but knowing his daddy, I'm sure not his last."

"Boy, this puts my wimpy prize to shame." Cooper loved the satisfaction and pleasure gleaming in her eyes as they traded stuffed animals. Not to mention how she readily reached for the ugly stuffed mongrel he'd won for her. "Where did you learn to shoot hoops like that?"

"I was a forward on my high school team and got through college on a basketball scholarship."

"Good thing to know if I ever challenge you to a one-on-one on the court," he said, then laughed as he managed to straddle Anthony's first carnival stuffed animal over the stroller handles. "You done showing off your skills, Ms. All-Star?"

Kelsey offered him a wink. "For now."

More determined than ever to get this lady into his arms, Cooper headed across the grass for the seating area at the edge of the already-crowded dance floor.

"Would you keep an eye on this stuff while I check out the little guy?" he asked, lifting Anthony from the stroller. "I'm sure he's in need of changing."

Kelsey nodded and Cooper disappeared into a nearby men's room, glad to find a pull-down changing table in the largest stall. Nice to know he wasn't the only dad who might be pulling diaper duty here at the fair. After taking care of business, he headed back to the table where he'd left his date only to find she was no longer alone.

Far from it.

His brother, Ross, and his wife, Julie, sat with her as well as Frannie while her husband, Roberto Mendoza, stood behind her holding their two-year-old daughter, Maribel, in his arms.

Cooper quickened his steps when he saw his sister lean toward Kelsey, her face and hands animated as she spoke. He was still too far away to hear what she was saying, but close enough to see the surprise that came over Kelsey's lovely face.

"Well, hello, everyone," he said as he joined them, Anthony held securely in one arm as he rested his free hand on Kelsey's shoulder. "Where did you all come from?"

His sister jumped to her feet so quickly Roberto put out his free hand to steady her, but Ross just leaned back in his chair and crossed his arms over his chest.

"Hey there, little brother." He tipped his chair back and peered at Cooper from beneath the brim of his Stetson with a wide grin. "Keeping out of trouble?"

Far from it.

Cooper glanced down at Kelsey's now-pink face. He'd managed to keep tonight fun and easy between the two of them. No talk of anything related to the future other than their plans for the next couple of hours.

Hell, he was still trying to figure how he was going to keep her with him after they got back to the ranch, but if his sister said something about his fool-headed confession the other day, "trouble" would be the least of his family's worries.

Chapter Eight

The warmth of Cooper's touch on Kelsey's bare shoulder made her shiver. He gave her a quick squeeze before he spoke.

"Oh, you know me, bro," Cooper answered Ross in a low drawl. "Trouble just seems to find me. Runs in the family, I think." He turned to his sister and added, "Isn't that right, sis?"

"Don't I know it." Frannie stepped away from her husband to reach for her nephew. "Hey, pass that cutie pie over to me."

Cooper did as she asked after dropping the diaper bag into the empty stroller. The baby went willingly, but Kelsey noticed the pretty blonde didn't meet her brother's hard stare when she took Anthony in her arms and held him close.

Was Cooper upset because his siblings had joined her while he was gone?

She'd been surprised when they'd called out to her and introduced themselves, having correctly guessed she was at the Spring Fling with Cooper. Turning down their request to sit with her would've been rude. Besides, they were nice, even if his sister had surprised her when she'd said—

Oh, my, was that it? Had Cooper overheard Frannie's comment?

"Would you like to take a turn around the dance floor?"

Kelsey looked up to find Cooper holding out his hand to her. He'd pulled his Stetson down over his brow, the smile gone from his face. She missed the flirty and carefree man she'd spent the last couple of hours with since initiating that kiss in the parking lot.

She'd assumed his silence during the drive to the fairgrounds was because he was as nervous as she was about tonight. Then she'd come up with the brilliant idea that sharing another kiss would take the edge off.

Not likely.

Being in his arms again had been amazing, as wonderful as the first time. Heck, even that quick peck last night at her front door had contained the same sizzle. And Cooper hadn't seemed to mind kissing her again. He'd made that very clear with the way his mouth had moved over hers, the desire in his eyes, and his body's obvious reaction.

Cooper started to lower his hand and Kelsey realized he took her silent daydreaming to mean she was turning him down.

She rose, sliding her fingers across his palm. "I'd love to dance with you."

His sexy smile was back and it once again reached his

eyes as he looked down at her, only to slip a bit when he turned to his sister. "Will you keep an eye on Anthony for a few minutes?"

"Of course," Frannie replied.

"I changed him, but he might be ready for a bottle. There are a couple in the bag I put together when we ate earlier—"

"Go on." His sister waved at the two of them as she sat again. "We'll be fine."

"Maribel is only just into her terrible twos. We still remember how to deal with one this little." Roberto sat next to his wife and balanced their daughter on his knee so she could see the baby. "You guys enjoy yourselves."

Gentle pressure against her lower back had her quickening her step. The heat of Cooper's touch through the thin material of her dress warmed Kelsey's skin.

"We're going to slow things down for y'all." The voice of the band's lead singer floated over the dancers. "So, gentlemen, take that special lady in your arms and enjoy yourselves."

"I like the sound of that," Cooper spoke in a rough whisper as he spun Kelsey around and pulled her into his arms.

"Me, too," Kelsey said, pressing her free hand into the strength of his shoulder, following his commanding lead. "I was hoping we'd get a chance to dance tonight. It's a good thing we ran into your family—"

He tightened his grip. "What did my sister say to you?"

His harsh tone surprised her. "Well, whatever it was, you don't sound too happy we spoke to each other at all."

"I'm sorry, that came out wrong," Cooper said, then sighed. "Geez, could I sound any more like a jerk?"

His apology had Kelsey hurrying to reassure him. "Your family was very nice. They simply asked if we were here together and where you and Anthony were."

Cooper nodded as he neatly turned them at the first corner. "My sister said something to you that—I don't know…you seemed surprised or embarrassed about when I came back."

Unable to look at him, Kelsey focused on the deeply tanned skin revealed by his open shirt collar. "It was nothing."

"Kels, come on. Tell me. Please."

Grateful for the dim lighting on the dance floor that hid the warm flush back on her cheeks, Kelsey said, "Frannie told me she'd deliberately asked someone to point me out because she had it on good authority— whatever that means—that you and I would be together tonight."

"Is that all?"

She shook her head. "She then said she wanted to meet the one woman in town who'd managed to snag a date with her very eligible, but confirmed-bachelor brother."

"Confirmed bachelor?"

Kelsey nodded. "It seems you are more of the keep-your-private-life-private-whenever-you're-in-town kind of guy was how she put it."

Cooper didn't reply even though some of the tension left his body. Suddenly, he moved out of the flow of dancers. A series of neat turns had them in the center area where other couples danced, slow and smooth, focused entirely on each other.

"My sister is right. I've never been on a date with anyone in Red Rock before. Until you." With a gentle pressure, he pulled her closer. The brim of his hat created a private cocoon as he dipped his head, his mouth at her ear. "I've never been interested before...until you."

Kelsey's insides melted at his sweet words. Unable to stop herself, she turned her face inward and whispered against his neck. "Well, I'm not sure how to take that. It's not like you've spent a lot of time in Red Rock."

"True, but I've been back a few times over the years to visit Frannie and spend time with Ross when he lived in San Antonio. Sometimes for a few weeks or a few months, but even then I pretty much kept to myself."

"And any extracurricular activities with the opposite sex...you kept those private, too?"

"Until you." He tucked their joined hands in close to his chest. "You know, I've wanted you back in my arms, just like this, for the last two hours."

The heated resolve of his words thrilled Kelsey. More than they probably should.

When his sister had emphasized Cooper's single-man status, a stab of trepidation had run through her. Getting involved with a man who had no interest in anything permanent seemed to be her pattern. Despite her claim of being interested in nothing but freedom, was she falling for the same type of guy yet again?

Maybe, but right now there was no place else she wanted to be.

"I've wanted that, too," she whispered.

The freshly washed scent of his dark blue shirt mixed with a rich, spicy cedar smell that rose from his skin. He rubbed his cheek against hers, his evening beard stubble gently scraping her jaw. One hand slipped low to her waist, their hips brushing as they danced. She tingled everywhere as his strength surrounded her and she had to hold back from leaning fully into him, very aware that if she did, she might not want to walk away.

As each song ended and another began, he kept moving in a timeless rhythm and she went along for the ride as time seemed to stand still.

"I wonder how many songs have played since we've been out here," he whispered.

"About four or five, I guess." That was a lie. She'd kept count and the fifth country ballad was coming to an end. Kelsey would remember the title of each song that had played tonight as he held her in his arms.

Cooper slowed to a stop, but kept his hand pressed against her lower back. He lifted her chin, making her look at him. Their eyes met and his head dipped slightly. Kelsey was unable to keep from wetting her lips with the tip of her tongue. Heated desire flared in his dark eyes.

He wanted to kiss her again. She wanted it, too.

The band swung into a fast country song and called out for line dancers to do some boot-scooting. The floor filled quickly with people jostling for position, and the moment was gone.

Cooper stepped away. "We should get back to Anthony."

Kelsey nodded and he let her take the lead back to the seating area. When she tried to release his hand, he tightened his grip, lacing his fingers through hers.

They walked hand in hand until it became impossible to stay attached. She pulled free as a group of teenagers filled the aisle, separating them. Spotting the stroller with the stuffed colt hanging over it, Kelsey smiled and headed toward it. She'd loved the look of surprise on Cooper's face when she'd sunk those baskets.

As she got closer, she noticed more people had gathered at the table where they'd left Anthony with Cooper's sister. In fact, the baby was now in the arms of—

"Where's Frannie?" Cooper was at her side again. "And who the hell is holding my son?"

"My mother."

"*Your* mother?"

Had he heard her right?

Cooper's gaze shot to the petite older woman with chin-length auburn hair trying to soothe his fussy boy. He picked up the resemblance between the two women immediately. They shared the same sparkly eyes and gentle but full-of-life smile.

"She and my dad came tonight with Jess and the kids, but I don't see Dad or my sister."

"Or mine. Frannie wouldn't leave Anthony with a stranger. Not that your mother's—" Cooper quickly amended. "You know what I mean."

She grinned at him. "Yes, I know."

Her amazing mouth captured his attention and Cooper had to force his gaze from her so as not to do something stupid. Like grab her and kiss her.

He scanned the seating area, looking for his sister. "So where did Fran go—ah, Lily's here. And there's Ross and Julie talking with JR and Isabella. Geez, our date night is turning into a Fortune family reunion."

"I think I liked it better when it was just you, me, Anthony and the carnival games," she said.

Kelsey's fingers brushed his shirtsleeve from his shoulder to his elbow before she tucked her hand into the bend of his arm. She leaned in and the now-familiar thrill at the feel of her curves against him shot through his body.

He slowed his steps to look down at her, covering her hand with his. "I *know* I liked it better when it was just me holding you close in my arms."

She blushed. "That, too."

The sun had set while they danced and dusk was closing in fast. Cooper hoped he correctly read the longing he saw in Kelsey's eyes. He planned to pick up where they left off on the dance floor later when they got back to his place and he'd put Anthony to bed.

"Good. Hold that thought."

Dropping her hand as they joined everyone, Cooper noticed the quizzical glances Kelsey's mother shot her daughter's way. He started to reach for Anthony, but Lily beat him to the woman's arms, flashing him a wink and smile as she offered to take his son. She then walked over to where JR and Ross stood talking with their wives.

"Hi, Mom." Kelsey leaned in and gave her mother a kiss on the cheek. "Where's Dad and Jess?"

"They headed for the Ferris wheel with the kids."

"So what are you doing here?"

"We were looking for you, but the grandkids couldn't wait. We ran into Frannie and Roberto. They said they were babysitting while you and Cooper danced."

Her mother's eyes shimmered with mischief as she looked directly at him before glancing at her daughter again. "Aren't you going to introduce me to the first young man who's snagged your attention since you got back to town? Despite the fact it meant you blowing off plans with your family?"

Kelsey blushed. "Mom, be nice."

Cooper had wondered about Kelsey's social life long before his sister ratted him out about his. Just because she'd made it clear she didn't date people she worked with, didn't mean there wasn't someone in Red Rock who'd been captured by her charms.

He took a step closer to his date and mentally filed away the older woman's comment. "Kelsey didn't tell me she already had plans when I asked her to come with me and Anthony tonight."

"A good-looking cowboy and his adorable son as opposed to hanging out with her parents? Not a hard choice."

Cooper liked her. He held out his hand. "Cooper Fortune, ma'am. It's a pleasure to meet you."

They shook hands and Cooper felt the scrutiny of a gaze only a mother could give. It'd been a long time since he'd met a date's parents. He immediately found himself wondering how he measured up.

"Jeannie Hunt," she replied, "and it's nice to meet you, too."

Lily walked back over to join them and Cooper quickly introduced the women to each other only to find out they had worked on many charity events together.

"So, Lily, what are you doing here?" he asked.

"Enjoying the Spring Fling like everyone else," she answered. "And no, William's not here with me. His doctor felt the crowds and noise would provide too much stimulation. Jeremy and Kirsten are staying with him."

She rubbed Anthony's back as she spoke, but his cries grew louder. "I took over watching Anthony for Frannie when their little one started fussing and they had to leave. She said to tell you he only finished a half a bottle. And speaking of stimulus, I think this little guy of yours has also had enough excitement for one night."

Cooper was already reaching for his son as she spoke, a rush of contentment filling him when Anthony burrowed into his shoulder. The baby's fussing quieted and Cooper placed his hand at the back of his tiny head. Anthony's skin was sweaty to the touch. "He feels warm."

"Do you think he's getting sick?" Kelsey asked.

Fighting back an initial rush of panic, Cooper focused on the two experienced mothers standing before him. "I…I don't know. Lily, Mrs. Hunt, what do you think?"

Both women placed their hands on Anthony when Cooper eased him away from his chest.

"He is a bit cranky, but perhaps he's just overexcited from being here," Kelsey's mother said. "And please, call me Jeannie."

"She's probably right," Lily added. "He's just ready for his own bed."

"Then we better head out." Kelsey reached for the stroller. "Why don't you just carry him? He seems calmer with you."

They said their goodbyes, Cooper getting his keys back from JR before they headed through the crowd. Anthony had quieted down by the time they reached the truck, but let out a wail the minute Cooper strapped him into the car seat.

"You probably want the rest of that bottle, but you're going to have to wait until we get home." From the swell of Anthony's cries and the whipping around of his tiny arms, his son wasn't too happy with that plan.

"Why don't I sit in the back while you drive?" Kelsey shoved the stuffed animals into the front passenger side of the truck. "The poor dear really wants to eat."

She didn't wait for him to reply.

Grabbing the diaper bag, she darted to the other side of the truck and crawled over the large wrapped package Cooper noticed lying on the seat. He realized it held the blanket he'd purchased for her from Isabella. JR must have put it inside Cooper's truck and then locked the doors afterward.

Kelsey ignored the package as she plopped down next to Anthony's car seat. Seconds later, she had the bottle out, gently shaking it before popping off the protective cap. The tears stopped and Anthony's eyes lit up as soon as he spotted what was in Kelsey's hands. He wrapped his chubby hands around it and latched on to the nipple, sucking noisily.

Cooper watched the two of them, chalking up his sudden inability to speak to Kelsey's quickness in fixing the situation. He'd been ready to deal with a crying baby all the way home. This solution never even occurred to him.

For someone who claimed a week ago that she didn't have a maternal bone in her body, she was amazing with his son. He was so damn glad she was here.

"Easy there, buddy," Kelsey said, as she leaned in close. Laughter followed, a low and husky chuckle that filled the truck cab. "You don't want to drown yourself."

The sound swirled through Cooper's chest and caused his heart to pound. He took a step forward, yanking off his hat when the brim knocked up against the truck's frame, wanting to be part of the intimate circle that was his son and this woman.

Say something. Say anything.

Thank her. Thank her for saying yes to your last-minute invite. Thank her for being smarter than you and easily finding a way to make things better for your son. Thank her for just being her.

Cooper tightened his grip on the back of the car seat and braced his other hand, still holding his Stetson, on the open truck door. He fought to catch his breath and regain his ability to form a coherent sentence. He felt like he was in a freefall, hard and fast. It scared the hell out of him that there was nothing he could do to stop it.

Kelsey and Anthony gazed at each other, and when Kelsey dipped her head even closer to smooth his brow with her fingertips, her hair fell slowly forward in a curtain of rich brown. The movement captured the baby's attention as well, and Anthony reached for the silky strands.

Cooper got there first and untangled his son's fingers before he could close them into a fist. "Oh, no, pal. You don't want to be doing that. We don't want to hurt the lady."

Kelsey glanced up at him for a long moment before she straightened and her hair slipped through his fingers. "Thanks," she said. "The hazards of long hair around a baby. I guess I should've worn it up in my usual ponytail."

Cooper tightened his grip, holding on to the last strands. It was crazy, but he didn't want to let her go. "I like it down."

There it was again. Despite an overhead truck light,

the cab's interior remained in inky shadows, but not dark enough that he couldn't see the deep yearning in those beautiful brown eyes of hers.

"Would you hold this for a minute?"

She had to repeat her question before Cooper realized she was talking about the baby's bottle.

He did as she asked and Kelsey lifted her arms, elbows angled out as she pulled back her hair in quick, smooth motions that pushed her breasts against the row of buttons down the front of her dress.

A deep rumble filled the air and for a second, Cooper thought he hadn't succeeded in holding back the groan that threatened to erupt from him. A second growl became a roll of thunder and a flash of bright light lit up the sky.

"Looks like we're leaving just in time," Kelsey said, lowering her arms, her hair now tied in a messy knot at the back of her head. "I didn't think it was going to storm tonight."

"Well, sometimes the unexpected just happens."

Cooper didn't know if he was talking about the change in the weather or his own internal whirlwind of emotions when it came to this woman.

"Why don't you get strapped in? I'll take care of the stroller and we'll beat the traffic out of here."

Exiting the fairgrounds, Cooper headed for the ranch and found his gaze straying continually to the backseat. Kelsey chattered softly to Anthony until Cooper drove the truck through the gates leading to Molly's Pride. By the time he pulled up to the front porch of his cottage, silence filled the truck.

Opening his door, he stepped into night air that felt thick and heavy in anticipation of the approaching rain.

Thunder rumbled across the dark sky, chased by long streaks of lightning. By the time he reached Anthony, Kelsey had already released him from his restraints.

"He woke up when you opened your door. Go ahead and take him," Kelsey whispered. "I'll get the rest of this stuff and bring it inside."

Cooper wanted to tell her not to worry about it, but if he did, would she just head to her apartment over the barn?

No, she wouldn't leave without saying good-night. And she couldn't say goodbye if he was busy with the baby.

He gave a quick nod of his head in agreement and lifted his son into his arms. Heading for the front door, he smiled when Anthony released a man-size belch as they entered. It was humid inside the house, so he left the door open for Kelsey and made a mental note to kick on the air-conditioning. He changed the baby's diaper, put him in a fresh onesie and laid him in his crib.

"Sweet dreams, little guy," he said, pulling a light blanket over his son. "And do your old man a favor and sleep through the night, okay?"

Walking back to the living room, Cooper watched Kelsey enter, her arms full of stuffed animals, Anthony's diaper bag and the wrapped package. She even wore his Stetson on her head. Pausing to allow the screen door to smack her in the backside before she fully stepped inside, he realized she was trying not to make any noise.

Still smiling, he moved to take everything from her except the package with her blanket inside. He dumped the animals and his hat on the dining room table and put the unused bottle of formula back into the refrigerator.

He returned to the living room in time to see Kelsey about to lay the package on the coffee table.

"Why don't you go ahead and open that?" he asked, moving in behind her. "It's for you."

She turned to look at him, her face in shadows. "Me?"

He nodded.

"Why would—what did you do?"

"Just open it."

She carefully worked at the plain brown wrapping, peeling it back slowly. A soft gasp escaped her lips when the multi-colored woven blanket spilled out. Picking it up, she held it out and looked at it for a long moment before clasping it to her chest.

"Oh, Cooper."

Damn, but he wanted to grab her and slam his mouth over hers every time she said his name like that.

"I saw how much you liked it when we stopped by Isabella's booth," he said instead.

A loud clap of thunder rang through the cottage and he looked down the hall, braced for Anthony's cries. When silence continued to fill the house, he turned back to find Kelsey had moved to the still-open front door.

"You shouldn't have done this." She stood with her back to him and stared out into the dark night, the blanket held close to her chest. "You didn't have to do this."

Three steps and he stood right behind her. "I wanted you to have a special reminder from tonight."

She shook her head. "Tonight was wonderful. I don't need—"

"Please, keep it." He reached out but didn't touch her. He curled his fingers into a fist and dropped his hand.

His skin burned like he was on fire. A fire that fed the fierce, pulsing ache he had for this woman. His clothes stuck to his body as his temperature soared. He fought not to grab her and pull her against him so she could feel the hard evidence of what his need for her was doing to him.

Instead, she turned to face him, her hair still held in place by that makeshift knot. He desperately wanted to see it loose and falling over her shoulders again. Taking a step closer, he dipped his head low to hers. The catch in her breath and the light sheen of perspiration on her skin had him curling his fingers at the damp nape of her neck.

He inhaled deeply, filling his head with her sweet strawberry scent as the words fell from his lips. "Stay with me tonight, Kelsey."

Chapter Nine

The moment Cooper spoke, the heavens opened. The pounding rain on the cottage roof matched the pounding of Kelsey's heart. Another round of booming thunder filled the air and she jumped.

His fingers massaged her neck while his thumb lightly trailed down her jaw to her collarbone. "Hey, it's only rain."

"I know." A gust of wind came through the screen door bringing a damp, cooling relief to her heated skin. "Oh, that feels good," she sighed.

He placed his other hand at her waist and pulled her closer, the folded blanket squashed between their bodies. "What feels good, honey? The rain or me?"

She looked up as bright flashes of lightning filled the interior of the cottage, allowing her to see the sharp contrast between his easy smile and the passion in his eyes.

Passion for her.

"Both."

His mouth crashed down on hers, taking the rest of her words as his hands moved across her lower back. She matched the thrust of his tongue with her own and a rush of cool air hit her upper thighs as his fingers curled into fists, bunching her skirt. She grabbed his upper arms, needing an anchor to hold on to as a powerful swirl of want and need churned through her.

From the moment they'd met, she'd known this would happen. As much as she tried to fight it, something deep inside her told her this was meant to be.

Cooper Fortune was the man she'd been waiting for.

Without lifting his mouth from hers, he released his hold on her dress and it dropped back into place. A moment later her blanket disappeared. She heard a light thud as it landed nearby. Then his hands were tunneling into her hair and angling her head to deepen the kiss.

He fought to free the long strands from the knot. The faint sting only heightened her desire. A deep groan escaped his mouth as he succeeded, the long locks gliding through his fingers to lie over her shoulders.

"Damn, I want you. But if you're not going to stay…" His words came in a jagged whisper as he slowly ended the kiss and stepped away from her.

He ran his hands down her bare arms until he reached her fingertips and even then, they gently tap-danced against the backs of her hands.

"Let me put that a different way. If you don't want to stay…to be with me, I'll crash out here on the couch and you can take my bed."

His words made her heart flip over in her chest. "My place isn't that far."

"It's raining, Kels."

"I won't melt."

He nodded, breaking contact with her completely and his keys jangled as he pulled them from his jeans pocket.

"Here, take my truck. Park it near the stairs and you'll be—" His gaze locked with hers as he held out the key ring. "Be inside your place in minutes. A little wet, but none the worse for the wear."

Oh, but she would be worse if she walked away from him.

She took the keys from his outstretched hand, watching the fractured disappointment cross his features. With a flick of her wrist, she tossed them over his shoulder, hoping they'd find a soft place to land.

Cooper wrapped his hands around her and pulled her up against him. "Tell me." His words filled her ear as he lightly sucked on the sensitive area of skin just below the lobe. "I need to hear you say it."

"I want you, too, Cooper." Her purse strap fell from her shoulder and she let the bag drop to the floor as she tunneled her fingers into his hair, saying the words aloud. For him. For her. "I want to stay. I want to be with you."

He took her mouth again in a ravenous kiss as he backed her up against the wall and pinned her there, his hips pressing into hers. The hard evidence of his arousal had her rising up on her tiptoes so she could cradle him at the juncture of her thighs. His hands moved to cup her breasts and she arched into his touch as more flashes of light illuminated the living room.

"The door," she gasped, pulling from his kiss. "Someone could see us."

Cooper nudged the front door with his boot, closing it. The loss of the cool breeze from the rainstorm ratcheted up the temperature inside the cottage.

"Oh, it's hot in here," she moaned.

"Baby, it's about to get even hotter."

He covered her mouth again in a carnal kiss as his fingers found the top button of her sundress. He slid the first one through the opening with difficulty. The second and third proved just as stubborn, but the feel of his calloused hands on her moist skin drove Kelsey crazy.

The longing to touch him in the same way made her blood boil as much as their dueling tongues. She tucked her hands beneath his bent arms. Mirroring his efforts, she easily undid the buttons on his shirt, not stopping until she reached the oversize belt buckle at his waist. She tugged his shirt open and placed her hands on his heated skin, nudging his hands and his mouth away to do so.

He slapped his open palms against the wall on either side of her head. A low groan filled the air as he held his body away from her, allowing her space to drag her hands from his flat stomach to his chest. She felt the hammering of his heart as she pushed his shirt off his wide shoulders.

"Damn, that feels good." Cooper rested his forehead against hers, his words coming with choppy breaths. "You're better at this than I am."

"Not really." She huffed as the cotton material caught on his sweat-soaked biceps and refused to budge. "This isn't going anywhere."

"Maybe I can help."

With one movement, he jerked his shirt free from the waist of his jeans and ripped it open, sending the last two buttons scattering into the shadows.

"Cooper!"

"Ah, much better." He tugged the material from his arms and dropped it to the floor. Then he placed his hands back on the wall on either side of her. "Now, it's your turn."

Her eyes had become accustomed to the room's dimness and she stared at the hard, lean muscles of his arms and broad chest. Her fingers traveled over scars that branded his skin, physical reminders of his years as a cowboy working the open range.

Unable to stop herself, she trailed her thumb over one mark that started just below his heart and snaked in a curve to his tapered waist. A sudden desire to follow that same path with her mouth had her tongue leaving a wet path over her top lip.

"Kels..." Restrained passion laced Cooper's voice as he drew out her name. "I said it's your turn."

She finally looked up at his face, having no idea what he was talking about. "Huh?"

"My hands are too clumsy for those little buttons of yours." He dipped his head toward her breasts. "So unless you want them to suffer the same fate as mine..."

His voice trailed off, and the promise of using the same method to free her from her clothing as he'd done to his own hung in the damp and muggy night air.

Another rumble of thunder from the still-raging storm crashed outside. She lifted her hands to the front of her sundress, praying he couldn't see how they trembled in the flashes of lightning that followed.

There were seven buttons to go, the last just below her belly button. Working slowly, two more buttons came undone before the lace of her bra peeked out. Cooper placed one hand on the swell of her breast and the heat of his touch caused a moan to slip past her lips.

She bit down on her bottom lip as his thumb grazed her nipple through the material. He did it again and again, pressing harder each time until he cupped her whole breast in his hand, and when his thumb and forefinger met, he gave her distended nipple a gentle squeeze.

Her hands stilled as she dropped her head back and groaned. "Cooper..."

"Don't stop," he whispered. "It's driving me crazy thinking of what you have on underneath this sexy dress."

"This isn't sexy. It's just a simple—"

"On you, everything is sexy."

She continued with the buttons, not stopping even when Cooper discovered the clasp to her bra between her breasts. He easily unsnapped it as the last button slipped free of its hold. He eased the dress and her bra from her, his palms brushing over her breasts before he pushed both items down her arms. They stuck to her and he had to tug them down over her hands. Her bra floated away, but it took a few quick yanks for the dress to make it past her hips and puddled at her feet on the floor.

He reached around her and cupped her bare bottom. He groaned again, louder this time, as one finger played with the tiny triangle of fabric at the waistband of her thong. "You were wearing nothing beneath that dress all night?"

"It's not…" she tried to speak, but the feel of his hands stroking her backside made it impossible. "It's not nothing."

"It's next to nothing."

And he loved it.

This had to be a dream. He'd been so sure she would walk out his door when she'd taken his keys, leaving him hard and hurting in his desire for her.

But the earthy, feminine scent rising with the heat of her body, her light touch on his skin, and the way she met his kisses, demanding and greedy, told him she was as turned on as he was.

Urgency throbbed through him as she pressed her almost-naked body to his. He traced the tiny straps of her underwear from her lush backside to her flat stomach as he lowered his mouth to one breast. She moaned as he sucked, tongued and teased, loving the sweet and salty taste of her skin. Her hands cradled his head then burrowed into his hair. When she directed him to her other breast, he willingly went and repeated his attention there, drawing the stiff peak into his mouth.

His fingers curled around the straps of her thong and he pushed the garment down her legs the same moment she reached between their bodies, releasing his belt buckle and freeing the top button of his jeans. Then the air disappeared from his lungs completely as she traced the thick ridge pressing against his fly.

Cooper lifted his mouth to suckle her neck, leaving a love bite as her fingers fumbled to find the small metal tab and then slowly lowered his zipper.

"I, ah… I need to tell you…" Kelsey's words came out in ragged breaths. "It's been a while since I've done… this."

He lifted his head and tried to concentrate on her statement, the effort was made only a bit easier when she slid her hands back up his chest. "Define a while."

"My last relationship ended…badly…a year ago. Tonight was the first date I've had since moving back to Red Rock."

He couldn't hold back as the corner of his mouth rose in a half grin.

"But you already figured that out."

"Yeah, I did." He lowered his mouth to hers and dipped his tongue in her sweet, wet heat once again before pulling back to nip at her full bottom lip. "It's been a while for me, too."

Her hands moved again, pausing to trace the scars he'd lived with for so long they were like old friends. He closed his eyes as her touch burned and soothed at the same time. How was that even possible?

"How long?" she whispered against his mouth.

"Almost a year and a half." A low chuckle broke free as a bright flash from the storm's lightning allowed him to read the surprise in her eyes. "What? You don't believe me?"

"No, I believe you."

"Good, because this first time might be kind of quick." His fingers moved through the damp curls between her thighs before he slid two fingers deep inside her. The rocking of her hips and the wet heat he found there told him she was ready.

"First time?"

"Oh, yeah." He flexed his fingers, drawing a deep moan from her. She clung to him, her fingernails biting into his shoulders as she lifted one leg, pressing her knee hard against his thigh as her shoe fell away. "But I'll make it up to you, I promise."

He wrapped his free hand around her raised thigh and tugged it higher on his hip. As much as he hated to do it, he pulled away from her and put his hand at her waist. "Put your other leg around me, too."

"Why?"

"So I can carry you to my bed."

She pressed frantic kisses against his jaw. "Is there anything wrong with where we are right now?"

He leaned back to look at her. "Here?"

"Right here, right now."

She let go of his shoulders and dropped her hands again, tugging on the open waistband of his jeans until they rode low on his hips and backside, his wide stance the only thing keeping them from going any farther. She reached past the smooth cotton of his briefs and freed him, cupping him in a firm grip before dragging her hand upward until her thumb danced over the wet tip.

"Make love to me, Cooper. Now."

He pressed her against the wall with his body, holding her in place as he captured her mouth in another blistering kiss. Making love to Kelsey had haunted his thoughts from the first moment he'd seen her. He'd always pictured them in the queen-size bed in his room, but he wasn't going to argue about location now.

He yanked his wallet from his back pocket, tore open the condom package and quickly sheathed himself. He lifted her off the floor, wrapping her legs around his waist as her other shoe joined the first on the floor.

She squealed in protest until he angled her hips and slowly entered her, the sweet sound turning into a moan as she broke free of his kiss. Her head dropped back against the wall in a soft thump as she rocked her body, pulling him in.

Denying the pulsating need to thrust deeply, Cooper fought for control as she tightened around him. Shudders racked his body as they surged together, over and over again, moving in perfect unison. Her breathing came in short, breaking gasps as he drove them higher and higher.

Damn, she felt too good, too perfect. He wasn't going to last. He felt her release moments before his own and he toppled over the edge of an unknown world where only the two of them existed. Her mouth reached for his and he took her joyous shout of pleasure into his soul. It was a long moment before he softened their kiss, lightly teasing, sipping at her lips. The power of their lovemaking drained the strength from him, but at the same time he felt like he could stay here forever.

The quivering of his leg muscles told another story, however, but he didn't want to leave her, didn't want to break this bond.

"Don't fall, Cooper."

Physically he was fine. Mentally? It might be too late as her soft words against his neck burrowed beneath his skin and moved downward until they branded his heart.

She started to lower her legs, but he tightened his hold, wrapping his arms around her before he took a step backward.

"Where do you think you're going, honey?"

"Cooper, you're shaking." She curled her arms around his neck and tightened her thighs at his waist.

"So are you."

Her husky laugh renewed his hunger and his body

responded. He walked into the bedroom, stopping to turn on the window A/C unit against the far wall. The rush of cool air bathed their saturated skin and they sighed in unison.

Kelsey dropped her head back and her hair blew free in the breeze. "That feels wonderful."

"Better than sex?" Cooper grinned at her, knowing the answering smile on her face was his doing.

"No, but at the moment it's a close second."

"Speaking of seconds…"

He lowered her to the bed, separating their bodies. She dropped her legs, her feet trailing along his jean-clad legs. He braced himself over her, willingly submitting as she tugged his head down to hers. Their mouths met in a lazy kiss that quickly surged from warm and content to bold and wanton.

Cooper pulled away, loving her soft whimper of disapproval at his retreat. "Get comfortable. I'll be right back."

He put himself back together, pulling his jeans back on, watching Kelsey as she scooted upward on the bed. She lifted her hips as her feet churned at the faded patchwork quilt and sheets beneath, dislodging them. "But not too comfortable, you hear? I plan to be naked when I crawl in beside you."

She rolled to her stomach and snuggled into one of his pillows. "Hmm, that's my plan, too."

Taking a few moments to check on his son, Cooper was glad to find the baby's skin cool to the touch. He then went out to lock the front door noticing the rain had slowed to a gentle shower and the thunder and lightning were gone.

He gathered their scattered clothes and cleaned up in

the bathroom, shedding his jeans, underwear, socks and boots before heading back to the bedroom. Closing the door behind him, he placed Kelsey's stuff on a nearby bench and tossed his into the corner. His last chore was clicking on the baby monitor next to his bed while his gaze roamed over Kelsey's naked back.

The snow-white sheets, pulled up to just cover the curve of her hip, were cool against his skin as he slid in next to her. He was more than ready to make love to her again, but as he leaned over from behind her and placed a kiss on her shoulder, he decided not to wake her if she was already asleep.

She wasn't, if the sexy arching that pressed her shoulder to his mouth and her backside against his hips meant anything.

"Hmm, whiskers…I like the way that feels."

Her voice was low and husky, making her sound like a woman who'd just been made love to, and loved well. She arched her neck and he took that to mean she wanted another kiss. He happily obliged, gently scraping his chin over her skin before reaching back to his bedside table. He palmed a small square package and placed it within reach beneath his pillow.

Propped up on one elbow, he lifted her long hair away from her back. He spread the long strands to the side across the pillow, loving how the dark color contrasted against the white bedding.

"I think you have a fanatical attachment to my hair," she mumbled, then sighed as he pressed his lips between her shoulder blades.

"I love your hair," he said between kisses, making his way down her spine, "and how your skin tastes like strawberries."

She remained silent for so long, Cooper started to wonder if he'd said something—

"More like salty strawberries by now."

He smiled, his grin widening when her hips lifted from the bed the moment he reached the curve of her backside. Gently sucking the tender skin into his mouth, he moved over her, sliding between her legs and bracketing his hands on either side of her body. She moaned as his mouth left his mark on her, an enticing sound that grew as he gently nudged her legs farther apart before he stretched out atop the length of her.

"Damn, you feel good beneath me."

Her response was to wiggle her backside against the hard length of him. Fighting for control, he kept his weight off her by using his elbows, then sliding his hands over hers, directing them upward until he wrapped her fingers around the wooden spindles that made up the bed's headboard.

"Don't let go, okay?" he whispered into her ear.

Her eyes remained closed as she nodded.

He drew his hands back, trailing his fingers along her arms to the soft sides of her breasts. Determined to take things slow, he rode the fine edge of control as he stroked, caressed and made love again to the beautiful woman in his bed, holding off his own powerful release until they shattered together.

Cooper woke the next morning facing the bedside table where the baby monitor sat. He'd found he was more receptive to Anthony's babbling or cries in that position. Then again, this was the first time he'd awakened in this bed with the press of soft curves against his back.

Not to mention fingertips making lazy circles over his stomach and a smooth leg lying over his. He laid a hand on her thigh and wondered for a moment if the two of them were going to experience any morning-after awkwardness.

"Good morning," he said softly.

A soft hum was her only response. He started to roll over, but she didn't move except to withdraw her hand until it lay flat against his back, her breathing low and even on his skin.

Was she still asleep?

They'd both drifted off after making love for the second time last night, but turned to each other once again just as the sun's rays broke over the horizon.

His mind wandered back to what had happened after that last time together. He'd held her in his arms until she'd drifted off. Restless, he'd gotten up and checked on Anthony, then found himself sinking into the rocker in the corner of the baby's room instead of heading back to bed.

Being with Kelsey last night—both at the Spring Fling and at his place—felt so right. For someone who'd always worked hard not to become attached, he found himself, and his heart, falling hard for the pretty horse trainer.

She was sexy, smart, fun, hard-working, close to her family and wonderful with his son. Wonderful with him.

So why the hell had he sat there for over an hour and thought about the past? Not just his history with women, but his childhood, too.

Growing up with a charming but self-centered mother had taught him all he didn't want in a relationship or in life. Hell, maybe he'd inherited those same traits. He'd been called both by past lovers, usually delivered with a slap to the face or a door slamming behind him on his way out.

Unable to come up with any answers other than a desire to be lying next to Kelsey again, he'd rejoined her, figuring the baby would be awake soon. Instead, he'd fallen into a deep, dreamless sleep.

Kelsey mumbled something he couldn't make out because at the same time a hushed cry echoed through the monitor and his stomach rumbled. Time for breakfast. Cooper eased from beneath the covers, blinking in the bright sunlight that streamed in the windows.

He looked at the clock, surprised to see it was almost nine. Kelsey burrowed into the pillows, so he pulled the blankets up to her shoulders. He'd feed Anthony first then fix breakfast for the two of them.

Pulling on clean briefs and a fresh pair of jeans, he scrubbed his hand through his bed-head hair and headed for the bathroom then the kitchen. He'd learned it was better to greet his son with a fresh bottle of moo juice than go into his room empty-handed.

Moments later, he found his five-month-old on his tummy doing the baby version of push-ups with a big grin on his face. Cooper laughed as he lifted him from the crib and soon had him in a clean diaper and undershirt. Nestling his son into the crook of his arm, he settled into the rocker as Anthony chugged on his bottle. Gently rocking, he enjoyed the quiet of the morning.

He didn't have to figure out everything right at this moment. It was enough that Kelsey was the first woman who made him want more. Want it all.

Anthony drained the bottle and popped the nipple

from his mouth with a happy gurgle. Cooper lifted him to his shoulder, and patted his back until the little guy gave a hearty burp right in Cooper's ear.

A sound so loud it almost drowned the click of the front door being opened, and then seconds later, closed.

Chapter Ten

"Going somewhere?"

Kelsey froze. Her hand still on the handle after she'd closed the front door instead of walking out like she planned. In her other hand were her purse and shoes while her arms held the beautiful blanket Cooper had given her last night—right before an amazing night of lovemaking that left her seduced, sore and serenely blissful.

She turned around. Her hair, done up in a loose braid she'd hastily crafted after Cooper left the bed—the second time—flew over one shoulder.

She zoomed in on his hair, mussed from sleep and finger combed, his naked-from-the-waist-up killer body, jeans faded in all the right places riding low on his hips and those sexy bare feet. Add the adorable baby cooing contently in his strong arms, much like she'd done last night, and she was seconds away from melting into a mess of feminine goo.

The only thing keeping her upright was the incredulity in his brown eyes. Eyes that had blazed with a passionate fire that all but consumed her, body and soul, last night.

"I know what this looks like," she said.

"And what is that?"

His clipped response had her straightening her shoulders. "I wasn't going to just leave."

He raised one eyebrow, the simple move telegraphing his disbelief.

"Okay, I was going to leave. I'm still leaving, but I changed my mind about doing so without saying goodbye first."

"You standing in my living room instead of out on the front porch is working in your favor." Cooper walked into the kitchen and placed Anthony into his high chair. He kept his back to her while making sure his son was properly strapped in. "And the fact that last night was incredible."

Incredible.

Amazing.

Marvelous.

Gee, she was a walking thesaurus when it came to describing making love with Cooper Fortune.

But now he was being distant as he moved to the kitchen counter putting together the baby's breakfast.

Not that she blamed him. Walking out the morning after without bothering to say goodbye was so...so... college-like?

He had every right to be upset, especially because he'd been so open and generous with her last night.

At least physically.

He'd shared his body with her in ways she'd never experienced with any man. A combination of the right words, whispered promises of exactly what he planned to do to her, and then fulfilling those promises with his hands, his mouth, his body.

Still, as much as she hated to say it, it felt as if he'd held a part of himself back, locked away.

She'd almost fallen back asleep when he'd left the bed after their third time together. He'd walked out of the room, and she'd lain there, listening, as the sun crept in. At first she thought he'd gone to check on his son, but then the steady creak of a rocking chair came through the bedside monitor—but no sound of the baby.

The minutes crept by and still Cooper hadn't returned. That was when she started to think about their night together and how he'd kept a part of himself separate from her.

Or was it...

Oh, no, was she the one who'd kept a distance between them even after a wonderful night together?

She'd worked hard to live up to her new motto of "free and easy" since the last jerk of a boyfriend had broken her heart, determined to live for the moment and enjoy herself without getting tangled up in a mess of emotions and feelings.

Then again, Cooper had made it clear his life before Anthony had been all about being a wandering cowboy with no connections, no responsibilities.

So why did he seem so upset that she'd actually thought about walking out with a goodbye? Was she breaching some kind of involved-but-not-connected rule she didn't know about?

"So, are you late for something?" Cooper's question pulled her from her thoughts as he yanked one of the dining room chairs close to Anthony's high chair and sat. "I had planned on fixing us breakfast after I filled this one's tummy."

Kelsey sighed. She didn't know if it was because he still wasn't looking at her or the magnificent view she had of his broad shoulders and naked back, but...

"Yes, I am late. Or I will be soon."

Okay, that got his attention. He looked at her over one shoulder before Anthony slapped his hands to the tray, demanding another mouthful of baby mush.

"You should have said something." Cooper returned to feeding his son. "I would've set the alarm. Or at the very least not kept you up so late."

"I'm sorry, Cooper. I should've told you I had to rush out of here after seeing the time." Kelsey walked up behind him. She desperately wanted to lay a hand on his shoulder, but from the sharp tone of his voice she doubted he'd welcome her touch. "I heard you in the baby's room and I didn't want to interrupt—"

Boy, that sounded so lame once she said it aloud.

"I didn't want there to be... I don't have a lot of exper—"

She bit hard at her bottom lip to stop the flow of excuses and moved to stand next to the baby so she was facing Cooper. One deep breath, and while releasing it, she let the truth fall from her lips.

"I've never had sex on a first date before."

The spoonful of fruit paused midway to Anthony's mouth and she finally had Cooper's full attention. He stared at her with those big brown eyes.

"Really?" he asked.

She nodded and the baby let loose with a sneeze that sent the contents of the spoon flying. Cooper swore softly underneath his breath and reached for a nearby rag.

"I know that sounds crazy—"

"No." He cut her off, his attention now on wiping down his arm and chest as well as the tray. "It doesn't sound crazy at all. So is that the reason you thought it'd be best to walk out, or do you actually have somewhere to be?"

"I'm going to church."

His gaze shot back to her.

Kelsey hurried to explain. "I meet my folks, Jess and the kids every Sunday for church services that start in less than an hour. Afterward, we go out for breakfast at this hole-in-the-wall place my parents have been going to for years that makes terrific pancakes. It's a family tradition."

Cooper stood, and even in bare feet he towered over her. He didn't look angry or upset anymore. In fact, his expression held no emotion at all.

Instinct told Kelsey to take a step back, but she held her ground. "You met my mom last night. They know we were on a date together. If I don't show up, they're going to think that I—that we—"

"You do know the words 'I spent the night in Cooper Fortune's bed' aren't stamped on your forehead, right?"

Her forehead? No.

Her heart? Kelsey was already afraid it was too late.

A heated blush crossed her cheeks. "I know that."

He looked at her for a long moment, but his steady

gaze revealed nothing. Anthony demanded his attention with insistent babbling, but Cooper continued to stare at her until he finally nodded, his eyes moving down to the blanket in her arms.

Kelsey tightened her grip on the material. "Okay, well...bye." She walked past him and headed for the door. Dropping her shoes, she worked her feet into them. "Oh, I found your keys this morning on the floor near the chair. I put them on the coffee table."

"Thanks."

Standing upright again, she yanked on the door handle, pulling it open. She reached for the screen door, and because she couldn't stop herself, she looked back. Cooper sat there, feeding his son. It was as if she'd already walked out.

So she did without saying another word.

"Boy, for someone who at times looked like a cat that swallowed the canary, you sure seem like you're about to toss that bird right back up here in the parking lot."

"Thanks, sis, what a sweet thing to say."

Kelsey watched her sister buckle the twins into the backseat of her car. Ella and Adam, Jess's other two kids, elected to ride home with their grandparents. Thankfully, they'd already headed out after the family breakfast that Kelsey barely remembered eating.

"Hey, you're the one who swung into the church parking lot like the devil himself was chasing you. Then you elected to sit between these squabbling two." Jess motioned to her kids through the rolled-up windows.

"You're the one who asked for help with Braden and Bethany."

"And when we headed inside the restaurant you

caught sight of that family," her sister kept talking right over Kelsey's feeble protest, "with the daddy holding junior in his arms—just like a certain cowboy we both know—and you got all dreamy eyed."

"I did not."

"Your seesawing continued all through breakfast. One minute you'd be lost in some far-off memory with a dopey smile on your face and the next you looked like you had to force down your cheese omelet."

Is *that* what she ordered? She hated cheese omelets.

"Good thing Mom and Dad were too busy playing referee for my misbehaving brood or I'm sure one, or both, would've been grilling you."

Kelsey reached into her purse and pulled out her keys. "I don't know what you're talking about."

"Oh, don't think you're getting away from me that easily."

Jess followed her around the back end of her blue minivan, and Kelsey realized her mistake in parking beneath the huge shade trees, because doing so had put her right next to her sister's vehicle.

"I need to get home, Jess."

Her sister tugged on her arm, swinging Kelsey around before she managed to open the driver's side door. "No, what you need to do is tell me how your date went last night."

Kelsey didn't have any idea what expression she had on her face, but if it was mirrored by her sister's, she was in big trouble.

"Wow, that bad?" Jess asked.

She shook her head, a smile coming to her lips as she remembered the carnival games and the dancing.

"That good?"

This time Kelsey nodded as the memories morphed into the moment Cooper had backed her up against the wall, the enthusiasm in his kiss knocking her right off her feet.

"You spent the night with him, didn't you?"

Kelsey nodded again, but dropped her head to hide her attempt at holding off the sudden appearance of tears.

"Oh, sis." Jessica stepped forward and slipped her arms around Kelsey's shoulders. "I'm hoping those are happy tears."

She returned her older sister's hug for a long moment then pulled back, brushing her fingertips over her cheeks. "They are, I guess."

"You guess?"

"We had a wonderful time at the Spring Fling. We ate, played games and danced."

Jess leaned against her minivan and crossed her arms. "Introduced him to Mom. Yes, she told me this morning. She thinks he's great."

"He is…great."

"So great that he's making my little sister cry? I might just have to pop him one in the nose."

The image of Jessica trying to land a right hook on Cooper made her smile. "There's no need to defend my honor. Everything that happened last night was mutual."

"As in mutually satisfying?" Jess asked. "Wait, don't answer that. From the expression on your face I'd choose the word…wonderful?"

"Add amazing and incredible and you might come

close," Kelsey said, repeating the words she'd used this morning to describe her night with Cooper to herself.

"So, what's with the gloomy faces this morning?"

Kelsey quickly explained how her original gut feeling that Cooper had held a part of himself from her last night had quickly morphed into the fear that she was the one who was holding back. Then she told what happened when she made the mistake of trying to leave without saying goodbye.

"Okay, so morning-after awkwardness happens all the time," her sister said. "And maybe you're not the free spirit you keep claiming you are."

"Yes, I thought of that, but you should've seen his face when I blurted out I'd never had sex on a first date before." She swept her hair over one shoulder. She'd thought about braiding it again after her hasty shower, but instead let it hang free. For reasons she didn't want to think about. "You would've thought he'd just defiled a virgin."

"It couldn't have been that bad. And you should've just given me or Mom a call and told us you were skipping services this morning."

Kelsey snorted. "Yeah, right. I'd have both of you at my place with a pot of soup and twenty questions."

"You're probably right. Look, maybe you're reading too much into this whole 'holding back' thing, be it you or Cooper. Maybe you were more upset with yourself because you were willing to sleep with someone you've only known a week. Not to mention on the first date."

Kelsey had come to the same conclusion under the hot spray of her shower this morning. "Maybe, but I still get the feeling his scars, both the physical ones and the ones I couldn't see, run deep."

"This guy's been through a lot in a short amount of time. From what you've told me, his whole world turned upside down when he found out about his son." Her sister gave her a gentle smile. "But it's you I'm more worried about. Your heart has been busted up by three different men, all of whom you thought loved you and were ready to commit to a life together. It's not surprising that you would pull back from those same emotions, especially since you've known Cooper such a short time."

Darn, it sucked when her sister made sense.

"So what are you going to do now? You're bound to run into him again. You're practically next-door neighbors." Jess leaned in close, her gaze sharp. "Even more important, where do you want this—whatever this is between you and Cooper—to go? Do you want to be with him?"

Yes.

Kelsey didn't even need to think about her answer. She wanted to be with Cooper, with Anthony, and find out if last night was a one-time experience or something more.

"Do I wait for him to come to me?" Kelsey asked. "Geez, that sounds so old-fashioned. And I was determined to be wild and free when it came to relationships."

"Take the first step. Fix him dinner."

"Dinner?"

"That old saying about 'the best way to a man's heart' still rings true." Jessica smiled. "Men love to eat and

Mom's fried chicken recipe always worked wonders on Dad. I used it a time or two on Pete."

"I don't even have his phone number."

"Do it the 'old-fashioned' way and invite him in person."

"Him and Anthony," Kelsey said, an idea springing to life inside her. "I'll fix dinner for the three of us."

It was midafternoon by the time Cooper returned home from another trip to the supermarket with a very fussy Anthony. Climbing up the front steps, he saw the note stuck to the screen door. His gut gave a little lurch at the thought that Kelsey might've been the one who'd written it.

Anthony let loose with another howl, so Cooper grabbed the folded piece of paper and shoved it into his pocket. Once inside, he got his son into a dry diaper and down for a nap. The hot afternoon sun made him thankful he'd passed up the half gallon of ice cream that would've been melted by now. Cooper got the groceries from his truck and put everything away before he remembered the note. He yanked it from his pocket at the same moment his cell phone vibrated on his hip.

"It's not her," he muttered. "You might've made love to the woman, but you never bothered to exchange cell phone numbers."

He opened the phone and pressed it to his ear. "Cooper Fortune."

"Hi, Cooper, it's Lily."

A sweet feminine voice, just not the one he longed to hear.

Cooper dragged his hand through his hair for what must be the thousandth time since Kelsey had walked out this morning. He moved into the living room and sank into one corner of the couch, only to rear up again when he realized he'd sat on the ugly purple stuffed animal he'd won for Kelsey last night.

"Hey, Lily. What's up?"

"I'm just calling to see how Anthony is doing. You seemed a bit worried when you left the fair last night."

"Anthony's doing fine," he said, tossing the animal to the next cushion. "He sneezed a few times today, but his skin is cool and he slept through the night. In fact, he's back in his crib for another nap right now."

"That's good to hear," Lily replied. "Did you have a good time last night? I saw you on the dance floor with Jeannie's daughter. You looked like you were having fun."

Cooper swallowed hard as the memory of holding Kelsey in his arms on the dance floor filled his head. "Yes, we had a very good time."

"I remember when William and I used to go dancing." Her voice turned soft and wistful. "I miss that. Of course, I miss the William we all used to know."

Cooper didn't know what to say to that, so he said nothing.

"And seeing so many Fortunes enjoying themselves at the Spring Fling gave me an idea," she went on, strength back in her tone. "I want to make this year's Memorial Day, well, memorable, for the entire family. I'm planning on having everyone out here to the ranch for a barbecue."

"Everyone?" He was surprised. That was a lot of Fortunes.

"Well, all of us who are in the area."

"Didn't the doctors say Uncle William shouldn't be overwhelmed?" Cooper asked. "You've been keeping his visitors down to two or three people at a time."

Lily sighed. "I know, but last night…"

He waited, but she didn't continue. "What about last night? Did something happen?"

"No, not how you mean, William's fine. He was already asleep when I got home from the fair. I sat in the chair in the corner of his bedroom, just watching him and praying for—I don't know. For something to tell me what to do to help him fully come back to us."

Damn, he had no idea what to say to that. "Lily, I wish I knew—"

"Shh, let me finish, sweetheart. Anyway, I must've dozed off because I dreamed about Ryan. Now, it might seem strange that I was at my fiancé's bedside and thinking about my first husband, but he told me William needed to be surrounded by his family. He needs to know we love him and support him, even if his memory never fully returns."

Her voice trailed off and silence filled the air between them.

"I can understand that," Cooper finally said.

"And this party won't just be for William's benefit. It's for Anthony, too."

"Anthony?"

"We need to celebrate the newest addition to the Fortune family." Lily paused for a moment, before she continued in a soft voice, "I believe creating new memories by welcoming Anthony officially into the family is just the thing for William, for all of us."

Cooper's throat closed up at the mention of the party being in his son's honor. There was no way he'd disappoint her. He cleared his throat and said, "Anthony and I'll be there. And let me know what I can do to help, what you need me to bring."

"Don't you worry about anything. Of course, you're welcome to bring Kelsey, too."

Cooper had no idea how things were going to be between him and Kelsey when they saw each other again, never mind asking her out for another date. "Okay, thanks."

They spoke for a few more minutes before Cooper hung up.

A party for his son.

He was stunned, but deep inside he knew he shouldn't be. The Fortune family was everything to Lily. She'd already proved her resiliency in doing whatever was needed to help William recover his memory, even if that meant taking divine advice from her first husband. From what he'd been told, Lily and Ryan had had a wonderful marriage until the man had passed away too soon from a brain tumor. The fact that she and his Uncle William had found love again with each other—

Hell, he'd never felt that way about a woman in his life. Never thought it was possible to fall in love, to want to spend his life with one person.

Until now?

He looked at the piece of paper in his hand. Flipping it open, he saw the small, neat handwriting. His gaze immediately went to the end to see who'd signed it.

Kelsey.

He released the breath he hadn't even realized he'd been holding and went back to read her note from the beginning.

Cooper,
I stopped by to see if you and Anthony are free for
dinner. I'll bring the food and I've got the perfect
blanket for a picnic. Around 5:00 p.m.? If you're
interested, give me a call.
Kelsey

Cooper grinned and punched in the number at the bottom of the note. It went to her voice mail. Damn, he hated talking to these things. Maybe he should hang up and call again later—

Beep!

"Ah, hey Kels…I got your note. I'm sorry I—ah, wasn't here when you stopped by. Yeah—yes, we'd love to have dinner with you…"

Beep!

Damn thing had cut him off midsentence. He was tempted to call her back, but was afraid he'd seem desperate if he did.

Well, wasn't he?

Cooper shut his eyes, his teeth clenching. Maybe, but that was a reality that was better kept to himself.

Chapter Eleven

Kelsey's knock came at ten minutes after five. Cooper halted his pacing, took a deep breath and glanced at his son who sat in an aptly named bouncy seat, waving his hands and feet at the colored beads attached to the handle.

"Wish me luck, kid." Cooper's words were a low whisper. "And let's hope your old man doesn't screw things up. Again."

He walked to the door and yanked it open. Kelsey stood on the other side of the screen looking exactly like she did the day they met. A simple T-shirt showed off her curves and snug jeans emphasized her long legs. Her hair was in a ponytail, but thankfully she'd left the ball cap at home, allowing him to see her beautiful eyes.

Eyes that stared back at him with a mixture of bravado and apprehension. Two feelings that were totally his fault, dammit.

"Kels, I'm sorry."

"Cooper, I'm sorry."

They spoke at the same time, their apologies jumbled together, then both smiled.

"I wanted to say it first." She shoved her hands into the back pockets of her jeans. "You beat me to it."

"I think it's a tie, but I'm glad we got that over with."

Relieved that getting things back to normal between them was that simple, Cooper pushed open the screen door. An oversize, wicker picnic basket, cooler and the blanket he'd given her sat next to her feet. "You want to come inside?"

She took a step back and jerked her thumb at the truck parked in front of the cottage. "Why don't I just put the picnic stuff in the back so we can head out?"

"I'll do that." He walked outside, and she again moved back, this time almost to the edge of the porch. "If you don't mind keeping an eye on Anthony?"

"Sure, no problem."

He held the door with a straight arm and Kelsey quickly ducked underneath and scooted inside. Maybe this wasn't going to be so easy after all. Minutes later the three of them climbed into his truck, but other than giving him directions to a shady grove of oak and ash trees near a small pond, Kelsey said very little.

"This is still part of Molly's Pride. I come here often when working the horses." She finally spoke, leaning out the passenger window when he eased the truck to a stop. "Wow, the ground still looks pretty wet. I figured with today's warm temperature and the sun…maybe we should go somewhere else."

Cooper had anticipated this problem when he'd read

her note. "No worries, I loaded the back of the truck with some extra blankets and pillows."

Enjoying the look of surprise on Kelsey's face, he parked so the truck's tailgate faced the water. He then hopped out, slapping his Stetson on his head.

Kelsey slid out, too. "But we can't picnic on the grass. Anthony will get—"

"We'll stay in the truck."

Cooper went to work making the truck bed comfortable, keeping the blanket he'd given her for last. Then he moved the cooler and basket off the lowered tailgate and set them into the middle of the blanket.

"There. One picnic, ready to go."

"I can't believe you thought of all this."

Hell, he'd pictured a similar scenario last night at the fairgrounds just before she'd kissed him.

A kiss he wanted badly to recreate, but instead he said, "Why don't you climb on up while I get Anthony from his seat?"

Kelsey nodded and bent to untie her tennis shoes.

He made quick work of freeing his son from the car seat. Grabbing the diaper bag, he turned back in time to see her scramble into the truck on her hands and knees. After she got settled up near the cab of the truck, he handed over his son and then joined them, stretching out his legs to keep his wet boots off the blankets.

He pulled in a deep breath, loving the fresh outdoor smell of Texas dirt, wild grass and the towering trees. The sky was a stark blue with not a cloud in sight and a slight breeze kept the late May afternoon from being too hot.

Bumping up the brim of his hat, he reached for Anthony, who showed his reluctance in leaving Kelsey by

grabbing handfuls of her shirt. *I know the feeling, kid.*
"Here, I'll take him."

She handed over his son and then pulled out a foil-covered dish from the picnic basket that had his mouth watering, a few smaller containers and a crusty loaf of bread.

"Can I do anything to help?" he asked.

He got a quick smile, but Kelsey kept her attention on the food. "You've got your hands full. I can take care of this."

Cooper pulled out a few toys for Anthony and watched as she set up a meal of fried chicken and potato salad. Call him crazy, but at the moment the last thing he wanted was food.

No, what he wanted was to lean over, cup her cheek until she finally looked at him.

Despite the limited space in the truck bed, she still seemed so distant. The couple of feet that separated them seemed bigger than the Grand Canyon. He wanted them back where they'd been last night—both at the fair and as they made love—but he was clueless how to get back into her good graces.

"Kels—"

"Okay, I think we're all set." She cut him off. "What do you want to drink? I brought bottled water, iced tea and I grabbed the last couple of beers I had in my fridge."

"Iced tea is fine."

"You sure? I kind of figured you for a guy who enjoys a cold brew."

"Not anymore. Not since Anthony came into my life. Too many memories of a mother who never quite learned her limit when it came to martinis."

Surprised that he actually said that aloud, he waited for a response, but Kelsey only nodded and handed him a cold bottle from the cooler. "Ready to eat?"

Not sure how he was going to get food past the lump of doubt in his throat, Cooper returned her nod. Setting the drink aside, he fixed a couple of pillows between them and propped Anthony upright, thankful the baby was content to play with a string of colorful beads.

After filling his plate, Cooper took a big bite of chicken, amazed when it did indeed slide down his throat. As soon as he could talk again, he said the first thing that popped into his head. "So, who's your favorite sports team? I'm guessing it's connected with b-ball?"

Surprise again crossed Kelsey's features, but he was genuinely interested. He knew she was great with horses, loved her family and had an awesome hook shot when it came to a basketball, but there had to be more to her. He wanted to know more, wanted to know everything.

Then they could work their way up to the hard stuff.

Like what had happened this morning.

They easily navigated some of the less complicated topics like sports and movies while enjoying the warm spring evening and keeping Anthony entertained. He discovered her passion for college basketball, and as a graduate of West Texas A&M, she was an ardent fan of the Lady Buffs. She also loved any film that included horses, with the classic National Velvet starring Elizabeth Taylor being her favorite.

"Thomas considered those two strikes against me," she said with a wistful smile, pushing around the remains of her salad with her fork. "That I played basketball and wanted to work with horses, but both were such a part of who I was—and I wasn't willing to give them up."

Cooper sat up a bit straighter. That was the first time she'd ever mentioned someone specific from her past. "I take it things didn't work with the guy?"

"Nope, and that's a good thing because otherwise I wouldn't be here with you two." She tossed the paper plate into a small trash bag next to her. "Of course, it's sort of a set pattern when it comes to the men in my life. Maybe that's why I'm more devoted to the four-legged stallions in my life than the two-legged ones."

Cooper smiled at her joke, but anger bubbled inside him that she'd been hurt like that. "Well, I love horse movies, too, but usually there's a cowboy or two involved."

"John Wayne or Clint Eastwood?"

Cooper handed over his empty plate when Kelsey motioned for it and grinned as he readjusted Anthony's pillows to keep the baby from falling over. "Gene Autry, actually."

"Really?"

"There was a run-down, one-screen movie theater a couple of blocks from where I grew up in San Antonio." He rarely shared this life-changing moment from his past, but after what she's just revealed about herself, it felt right. "The summer I was twelve, they showed Gene Autry Westerns every day. I saw as many as I could, two or three a day sometimes."

Kelsey froze in the middle of putting away the remains of their picnic dinner. "Your folks didn't mind you spending all your time and money at the movies?"

Hell, that summer hadn't been any different than any other.

He shrugged and kept his attention on the horseshoe-shaped baby rattle he spun in a lazy circle with his finger. "My dad had been long gone by then and my mother all but disappeared with her latest boyfriend. My older brother, Ross, was in charge of keeping me and my siblings out of trouble."

"Oh, Cooper."

"Seeing how I rarely had any money, I found a way into the theater through a busted window." He continued talking over her sympathetic tone, having no idea why he was saying all this, but the words spilled out of his mouth anyway.

"It worked pretty well until I got caught by the owner, but instead of calling the cops, he gave me a job. So, I made a few bucks under the table and saw all the movies I wanted for free. I knew then what I wanted to be when I grew up."

"A cowboy."

He nodded, remembering how he'd spent the following summer in Red Rock at his Uncle Ryan's ranch learning all he could about horses and the hard work involved with his dream job. By the time he'd graduated from high school he'd been working at a local ranch and entering rodeos.

"That must've been rough, being on your own that summer."

"Did you know there's even a Gene Autry Cowboy Code?" he asked, switching the conversation back to a more neutral topic. "I used to know it by heart when I was a kid, something about always telling the truth, being gentle with children and respecting women."

"I think you live up to that code pretty well."

That was nice to hear, but if he was telling the truth

at the moment it'd be that he wanted nothing more than to pull her into his arms. No, that wasn't entirely true, either. He wanted to do that and so much more, but if she knew that, she'd probably kick his ass right out of the truck. Things were finally relaxed between them.

Did he really want to screw that up?

"Well, I guess we can thank the movies for our careers, huh?" Kelsey said. "Funny how both of us ended up following our childhood dreams."

Except Cooper's dream never included being tied down. Thanks to his mother's life choices, he'd always believed having a spouse and children wasn't worth the time, effort or required commitment, but taking care of his son wasn't any trouble.

He'd willingly admit there'd been a big learning curve involved at first, but he was getting the hang of this parenting thing. He glanced down at Anthony who let loose with a big yawn and rubbed at his eyes with tiny fists.

Yeah, he liked being a dad.

Holding his sleepy son in his arms as he sucked down the contents of his bottle, Cooper decided that once Anthony settled down for a nap he was going to do something drastic.

Like grab the woman and kiss her. Or give her the kind of apology she deserved; whichever came first.

After Anthony made it clear he was more interested in sleeping than eating, Cooper put the half-finished bottle away and gently laid his son in a cocoon of pillows, the little guy's eyes already closed. He reached for the light blanket nearby, but Kelsey got there first and covered him.

"They're so sweet when they're sleeping," she

whispered, lightly caressing Anthony's cheek with her fingers. "Just like little angels who've fallen from heaven."

"Yeah, sweet." A heavy feeling settled in his gut as he watched her, remembering that dim-witted line he'd spouted off to her that first day. The thing was she really did remind him of an angel.

"You're good with him."

Kelsey's soft praise hit him square in the chest. He blinked and looked down as Anthony coughed and snuffled, rubbing at his nose in his sleep.

"Thanks. Considering I've had a crash course in this baby stuff, I don't think I'm doing too badly. Not that I still don't have doubts, but I really think I can handle this daddy business." Cooper leaned back, put his weight on one arm and patted his stomach with his free hand. "And thanks for a great dinner. I'm stuffed."

"Does that mean you're not interested in a tasty dessert?"

Yeah, he was, but he doubted his idea of dessert, as in her mouth under his, was what Kelsey had in mind.

He watched as she took out a trio of bright green apples and a plastic dish filled with a dark brown liquid. Then out came a paring knife and in minutes she skinned one of the apples entirely without stopping.

"Okay, I'm impressed."

Kelsey blushed. "It's not that big of a deal."

"I've never met anyone who can peel a whole apple in one long curl," Cooper said. "And with such speed."

"Well, now we both know you're easily entertained." She sliced the apple into pieces and then took the lid off the container. Using a spoon to first stir the contents, she then dipped in an apple slice.

Cooper peered at the bowl. "What is that?"

"Melted caramel. Do you want a piece?"

He should've known.

He'd learned last night how much of a sweet tooth she had. Cooper shook his head and watched as she quickly placed the apple in her mouth, using the tip of her tongue to catch the gooey strings that followed. "Mmm, so good."

She ate two more bites, needing the help of her fingers to stop the messy liquid from dripping down her chin. His smile faded as she slowly licked the sticky remnants from her fingers. The sight of her lips closing over each individual tip drove him crazy.

Damn, she was killing him.

"Okay, now I get it."

The last caramel-covered finger stopped inches from her mouth. "What?"

"This is divine punishment, right? When I couldn't think about anything except how much it hurt that you'd planned to walk out on me."

"Cooper—"

"No, I totally understand."

It was time to man up and just spit it out.

He wanted to be with this woman and it was time he told her so. He yanked off his hat, needing to see her eyes as he spoke. "I'm sorry, Kels. I was a total ass this morning. I never even thought about how you might be handling—" he paused and waved his hand between them "—whatever this crazy thing is between us. All I could think about—still think about—is how amazing last night was, and I'm not just talking about when we got back to my place—"

She leaned over and pressed her fingers, including the sticky caramel one, to his lips. "Cooper, shut up."

He did as he was told.

Then he captured her hand when she started to pull away. Drawing her finger into his mouth, he gently sucked the sweet confection from her skin. Passion blazed in her eyes, the same passion he'd seen last night when she looked at him as he made love to her.

He curled her hand in his. "Would you believe me if I told you I had to kiss you right now or I'm going to die?"

Ah, a smile.

"No."

His heart stopped. "No, I can't kiss you?"

Her smile turned soft yet sexy and his ticker started pounding again. "No, I don't believe you."

He scooted closer. "Are you willing to take that chance?"

"No," she repeated.

He covered her mouth with his. Pressing her hand to his chest, he slid his to the nape of her neck and held her like he'd wanted to ever since she'd appeared on his front porch. The way he should've kissed her the moment she'd told him she'd never had sex on a first date before.

Delving into the warm wetness of her mouth, he tasted the tartness of the apples mixed with the remaining sweetness of the sugary caramel.

"Come home with me," he whispered against her lips.

She eased back but didn't answer as she focused her gaze on the container of melted caramel in her lap. He tipped her head up until she looked at him again, using his thumb to free her bottom lip from where she'd captured it with her teeth.

"What do you say? We'll get Anthony down for the night and then watch a movie or something."

"Or something?"

He grinned, feeling like a teenager trying to get a date to hang out at his house, or would've if he'd ever been crazy enough to ask a girl back to his childhood home. "Come on, we'll pop popcorn, open a bottle of wine and find a classic film featuring horses."

She stayed silent, staring back with an expression he couldn't read. Didn't she want this, too? Or was the combination of him and Anthony too much for her? She was so good with the baby, but maybe that was because of her bond with her sister's kids.

Maybe she wasn't willing to spend time with a man who came as part of a package deal. But that didn't explain why she'd agreed to go on a date with him and Anthony in the first place. Or why she'd left that note asking them to go on this picnic.

"Look, things started backward between us—making love first and talking about dating now. Hell, it worked when it came to fatherhood. Maybe it'll work for us, too?" He lowered his forehead until his rested against hers. "I want to be with you, Kelsey. I want us to be together. We can take things as fast or as slow at you want. How does that sound?"

Wonderful.

It sounded wonderful, because she wanted that, too.

Kelsey hadn't realized how much until just now when Cooper had put his feelings into words. Words she should've said first, words she'd wanted to say from the moment he answered his front door and blurted out that sweet apology.

Yes, it was scary, getting involved with someone again. And this time it wasn't just one someone. Falling for a single dad came with a whole separate set of emotions and concerns that only heightened the risk she'd be taking. After her engagement ended six years ago she'd only been involved with a couple of men, and all of them had been free from the responsibility that having a child in your life required. Was she ready to take on a relationship that included three hearts instead of two?

Cooper was willing to take a chance.

He'd just said so.

"I want that, too," she said softly, cupping his face with her hands. Her gaze flitted over the T-shirt that couldn't hide the well-defined muscles of his chest and shoulders, to the jeans molding themselves to his legs. She quickly looked him in the eye again. "I want to be with you."

Cooper lifted the plastic container from her lap, replaced the lid and set it to one side. "No sense being messy about this."

"About what?"

"This."

He gathered her into his arms and pulled her close until she was practically lying on his chest. She panicked, not wanting to squash Anthony, but Cooper's hands bracketed her hips, holding her in place. His mouth met hers and his kisses were fervent, yet gentle. Powerful, yet hesitant, almost as if he was afraid to show her the same passion and fire as they'd shared last night.

She wanted that fervor, and tried to tell him in her kisses, but the sound of Anthony coughing again broke through, reminding her now wasn't the time or the place.

"Hmm, it's getting cooler now that the sun is about to set. Maybe we should get this little one home." Kelsey pulled away, her hand on Cooper's chest. His heart thumped hard beneath her touch. "And us, too."

"I like the sound of that."

The low-timbered seductiveness of his words made her smile.

Two days later, Kelsey was still smiling.

Other than spending her daytime hours working with her horses, every spare moment was spent with Cooper and Anthony. They'd made popcorn and found a movie with horses to watch Sunday night after giving Anthony a bath and getting him to bed. A contemporary-cowboy-meets-city-girl story based on a romance novel. Her smile widened. She never got to see the ending of that film thanks to Cooper's persuasive, butter-flavored kisses.

Monday morning started with breakfast in bed that almost made her late to work, and the evening ended with the three of them having dinner out at Red, where they'd run into everyone from Cooper's cousins to her parents. When Anthony's coughing persisted, they returned early to the cottage and enjoyed another night in each other's arms.

Today she'd spent most of the day at a neighboring ranch picking up a couple more horses, and now she was hurrying through her shower as they again had plans.

She rinsed off her strawberry body wash, willing

away the memories of this morning's exploits in Cooper's shower that started with her surprising him under the hot and steamy spray.

"Girl, you are just too darn happy," Kelsey said aloud to no one, then giggled.

Oh, man, she was losing it. She'd never felt so giddy in her life, even when flying wild and free on the back of one of her horses. Over the last forty-eight hours, she and Cooper had talked, laughed and shared stories about their lives.

She'd spoken freely about cherished childhood memories of family holidays, summer vacations and when her parents surprised her on her thirteenth birthday with her first horse, who she named Cupcake.

Most of Cooper's stories revolved around his brothers and sister, rarely including his mother or any adult except for the times they'd spent at the Fortune's homestead, the Double Crown Ranch. He talked about leaving home after he turned eighteen having decided at such a young age that being part of a family was too hard to deal with and how that same attitude stayed with him over the years.

He'd talked about his drifter-inspired lifestyle, his eyes taking on a faraway look as he spoke of the sunsets he'd witnessed all over the country, but he really seemed to enjoy the scrapbook she'd shared with him, a book her mother had created for her that detailed every birthday celebration from her first to her eighteenth. After flipping through the pages, Cooper had grown quiet, saying that Anthony was closing in on being six months old and he didn't have one photograph of his son. A shortfall he planned to remedy by going camera shopping today.

Boy, when the man saw a problem, he went right to work fixing it. That was one of the things she loved—

Kelsey cut off that thought abruptly as she twisted the shower knobs, turning off the water.

Nope, not going there.

Only ten days of knowing this man and she was ready to use the "L" word?

Cooper Fortune was a fascinating and charismatic man and a great father. He was also a man who carried a lot of baggage from what she gathered was a very unhappy childhood, a childhood that must have left scars as deep inside him as those decorating his skin.

And she had to admit he wasn't the only one with scars.

Her sister was right. The men she'd been involved with in the past had done quite a number on her heart. As wonderful as things were between her and Cooper, she had to take things slowly.

Wrapping her hair turban-style in a towel and grabbing a second one to dry off, she entered her bedroom in time to hear her ring tone touting how her heroes had always been cowboys. She hesitated for a moment, then grabbed her cell phone.

"Hey, handsome," she answered, knowing it was Cooper. She kept her voice light and flirty, determined to get her happy outlook back in place. "You caught me fresh from the shower."

"How fresh?"

She grinned. Just the sound of his voice, and her attitude was adjusted. "Birthday-suit fresh."

A low groan filled her ear. "And you're way over there and I'm here."

Kelsey eyed the baby-blue satin bra and panties on

her bed. "Well, let me slip into a little something and I'll be with you in a few minutes."

"I would say clothing is optional," Cooper replied, "but I'm in need of a different kind of favor right now."

Chapter Twelve

"Hmm, now I'm intrigued." Kelsey lowered her voice to a husky whisper. "What's my assignment?"

Cooper's guttural laughter filled the earpiece. "Nothing covert. I know we had plans for an adults-only night with dinner out and a movie, but I think I need to stay home instead."

Disappointment coursed through Kelsey. "Did something happen today?"

"Yeah, Anthony's fighting a cold, so I thought it'd be best if we stayed in. How does a pizza and a DVD sound instead?"

Like heaven, as long as she was with Cooper.

"Sounds great. I'll run into town." She dropped her towel and wiggled into her panties while cradling the phone between her ear and shoulder. "Is Anthony running a fever?"

"No, thank goodness, but don't ask how many times

I had to read the section in the baby book on the proper method for taking the temperature of a five-month-old, via the back end no less, before I was brave enough to try."

At the cringe in Cooper's voice, she fought to keep the humor from hers. "Can I ask how many tries it took to get the feat accomplished?"

"No, and I don't know who was more traumatized, me or him." Cooper paused for a moment, then continued. "But his coughing and sneezing have gotten worse and his nose is all stuffed up. I called the clinic and spoke to a nurse. She recommended saline drops and a baby nasal aspirator. Do you have any idea how those two things work on a five-month-old?"

"Sorry, no clue."

"I'll enlighten you when you get here. It's more fun than video games."

Kelsey laughed and promised to be there soon. After hanging up, she finished dressing and called the pizzeria in the center of town. Twenty minutes later she headed back to Molly's Pride with the mouthwatering aroma of melted cheese, hot tomato sauce and spices filling the interior of her car.

She parked outside the cottage and grabbing the pizza, made her way onto the porch. "Knock, knock," she called through the screen door. "Pizza delivery."

Cooper met her at the door with a fussy baby in his arms. He gave her a quick kiss, one hand running the length of her hair. "Hmm, a wet head. Just how fresh from the shower were you?"

"Dripping wet and wrapped in a fresh towel." Kelsey moved past him and put the pizza box on the coffee table. "What did you think that was? Phone sex?"

"With the way this little one is feeling tonight it might be as close as we get."

Taking an elastic band from her wrist, she tamed her hair into a high ponytail. Cooper was watching so she gave him a quick wink and then held out her hands. "Aw, come here, Anthony. Are you not feeling good?"

"I think it's been building over the last couple of days." Cooper handed over his son and walked to the kitchen. Returning with two sodas and a couple of plates, he placed them next to the pizza. "We should probably eat before I demonstrate the nose thing. It's not pretty."

Kelsey noticed the gunk built up around Anthony's nostrils. "Hmm, I think we might have to tag team on dinner. You go first while I keep this little guy busy. Do you have a damp, soft cloth?"

Three hours later most of the pizza was gone.

Anthony had finally settled down, more from exhaustion than anything else, Kelsey suspected. It took a warm bath, a lot of pacing and the two of them taking turns rocking the baby before he finally gave up the fight and closed his eyes.

Cooper had sat in the rocker with him for the last half hour just to make sure his son was asleep. Kelsey stood in the doorway, watching him as he held Anthony to his chest, one large hand spread wide on the baby's back. When he'd turned his head and pressed a soft kiss to Anthony's temple, it felt as if her heart tumbled right out of her chest and landed at her feet.

When it finally returned to its rightful place, she heard a different rhythm. A harmonious tempo she'd never experienced before in her life.

I belong to Cooper.

The six-beat cadence matched the words dancing in her head, telling her it was time to face the simple truth. She was in love.

Like a tender breeze or a soft rain, the emotion enveloped Kelsey. The potency and sureness of it was so surprising she had to lean against the doorjamb, her ability to stay upright suddenly in jeopardy. Her heart was telling her what her head refused to accept.

She was head over heels in love, and not only with Cooper Fortune, wandering cowboy and new dad, but with Anthony, too. Father and son, a package deal.

Oh, what was she going to do now? How was she going to tell him? Cooper had said they would go as fast or as slow as she wanted, but Kelsey doubted he'd meant falling in love in less than two weeks. In just over two days of officially dating.

Cooper slowed the motion of the rocking chair and rose. He looked so strong and sure and safe, cradling his son in his arms. In the soft glow of the night-light, he caught her watching him, and smiled.

At that moment, Kelsey realized that trying to put a timeline on what she felt was impossible. The love was there, as physically powerful as the man standing before her.

Two weeks, two days, two hours. It didn't matter. She loved Cooper and his child with everything in her.

He crossed the room and laid Anthony in his crib. The little guy's breath was ragged, but thankfully he continued to sleep. Gripping the railing, Cooper stood there, watching his son. Worry mixed with joy on the sharp angles of his face, both emotions reflecting the strength of his connection to someone who'd only been in his life for a short time.

Then suddenly he was there, right in front of her. Tummy clenching, she scooted back into the hall and he followed, stopping her from going any farther by pulling her into his arms. She melted into his embrace, pressing her cheek to his chest, loving the heat of his touch and the steady beat of his heart.

They stood in the quiet of the night, and Kelsey realized that while she couldn't control her feelings, she could decide where and when to put those feelings into words. There would be plenty of time to find the right moment to tell Cooper how much he meant to her, but until then, she'd hold the precious sentiment deep inside.

"I'm beat." Cooper leaned back and looked at her, his voice a low whisper. "I know it's only ten o'clock, but I'm ready for bed. Do you want to stay tonight?"

Kelsey loved how he always asked, never assumed, that she'd stay and share his bed. Being with him meant getting up early and heading back to her place in order to get ready for work, and while none of the other ranch staff had said anything, they had to know about the two of them.

But that didn't matter because there was no place else on earth she'd rather be than right here.

She nodded and they moved into his bedroom, not bothering to turn on any lights. They stood at his bed-side and he tilted her chin up with his fingers and gently kissed her lips. A kiss that deepened quickly and soon they were undressing each other with frantic hands. She slid beneath the covers as Cooper made sure the monitor was on. Then he crawled in next to her and again pulled her into his arms.

"Now what can I do to thank you for coming over,"

he murmured into her hair, "and for being so wonderful with Anthony tonight?"

She tangled her legs with his and slowly drew her hand up the length of his arm to his shoulder. Placing her lips at his neck, she kissed along the length of his collarbone. "Hmm, I don't know, cowboy. What did you have in mind?"

Cooper gently rolled over until she was flat on her back beneath him. "You know, I never paid you for picking up dinner tonight."

"That's okay." She tunneled her fingers into his hair and tugged until she felt his smiling lips on hers. "I'll take it out in trade. If you're sure you're not too tired."

"Who, me?"

"Kelsey?"

Somewhere between sleep and consciousness, she heard Cooper calling for her. His voice carried through the baby monitor. He was in Anthony's room. Jumping out of bed, she stumbled into the hall, tugging the T-shirt she'd pulled on sometime during the night past her hips. He called her name again as he joined her. This time there was an edge of panic in his tone.

"I'm right here, Cooper. What is it?"

He headed for the bathroom, Anthony in his arms. "He's not breathing right."

She followed, hearing the baby's rapid, labored gasps. "Did you do the syringe thing on his nose?"

"Yes, but this is different. It's as if he's not getting enough air into his lungs. Here, take him." He placed his son in her arms. "I'm going to get the hot water running in the shower to get some steam in here."

She held Anthony close and checked for a fever. He

didn't seem to have one. She placed a hand on his tiny chest, concern knotting her gut as she felt his struggles to breathe. "How did you know about the steam?"

"From the baby book I've been devouring the last few weeks. The steam should help."

Moments later, the room filled with warm, moist air. They stood huddled together as the minutes ticked by. Anthony's fussing grew, his cries throatier and deeper, making it even harder for him to catch his breath.

"Maybe you should call the after-hours number at the clinic? Or call Jeremy?" Kelsey forced her voice to remain calm, her heart breaking over what the little guy was going through. "Tell him what's happening and see what he suggests we do."

Cooper studied her for a long moment before he nodded and left the bathroom, closing the door behind him to keep the steam inside. Swaying in a gentle motion, she tried to soothe the baby with nonsense babbling, but Anthony's distress only increased.

Ten minutes later, Cooper returned. The first thing she saw was the fear on his face. Then she noticed he'd traded his sweatpants for a T-shirt, jeans and his boots.

"I need to take him to the emergency room."

Kelsey froze, that one sentence causing her heart to seize in her chest. "At the clinic?"

Cooper shook his head as he reached into the shower and shut off the water. "San Antonio."

"Give me a second to change and we'll go."

He took Anthony from her. "You don't have to—"

"Of course I do." She brushed past him, already lifting the T-shirt over her head. "Go ahead and get him into his car seat. I'll be right there."

The trip to the city was a blur.

After hearing Cooper's description of Anthony's struggle to breathe, the doctor had recommended they take him directly to Children's Hospital, twenty miles away. Jeremy had called back during the ride to tell Cooper that he had a good friend, a pediatrician, on staff at the hospital. Dr. Jason Stanhope would meet them at the hospital's emergency room. Jeremy was also heading in and would meet them there.

Thankfully, the roads were empty, given that it was almost two-thirty in the morning. It killed her to sit next to Anthony and listen to the child struggle for his next breath. She tried to keep him calm as the unbridled fear of the unknown raced through her.

They parked near the entrance and raced inside. A doctor in green scrubs, looking freshly awake, greeted Cooper by name and ushered him and Anthony through a set of large swinging doors.

"Excuse me, miss, are you the baby's mother?"

Kelsey stopped and looked at the young nurse who was barring her from following Cooper. "No, I'm...I'm not."

"I'm sorry. It's family only past this point." Her smile was kind, but her voice was firm. "You'll have to wait out here."

Kelsey watched Cooper stride down the hall, Anthony in his arms as he spoke to the doctor. He never looked back, never noticed that she wasn't with him.

Shaking off her self-centered concern, she entered the waiting area, but its quietness didn't help Kelsey's overactive imagination. She tried to sit, flip through the old magazines but ended up pacing the length of the room while a television turned to a twenty-four-hour news station droned in the background.

Unable to stand the silence and not knowing what was going on, she walked over to the check-in desk. "Excuse me, I came in about twenty minutes ago with a man and baby. Can you tell me anything about how he's doing?"

"What's the name?" The nurse asked.

"Fortune. The baby is Anthony Fortune."

Kelsey noticed the woman's raised eyebrows in response to Cooper's family name, a name that carried a lot of weight in this part of the state.

"Are you a family member?"

"No, I'm...I'm a close friend of Cooper Fortune, the baby's father. He's back there with his son."

The nurse, who didn't look much older than Kelsey, offered an apologetic smile. "I'm sorry, I can't tell you anything other than he's still being checked by the hospital staff."

She should've known that would be the answer. "Can you at least tell me if Dr. Jeremy Fortune has arrived?"

The nurse's fingers flew again over the keyboard. "Yes, he's here, but that's all I can say."

"Thank you."

Kelsey moved out of the way for a young couple with a toddler in their arms, and went back to the waiting area. A part of her was glad that Cooper had someone with him. She was surprised Kirsten, Jeremy's fiancée, hadn't come with him, but maybe she had? Maybe she was back there with Cooper and the baby. Kirsten wasn't family yet, but perhaps Jeremy had pulled some strings to get her past the large gray doors.

Running her fingers through her hair, Kelsey stared at those doors, praying Cooper would walk through and tell her what was going on. Tell her that Anthony was going to be okay.

She looked at her cell phone. Forty-five minutes since they'd arrived and still no news. Was that good or bad?

More people of all shapes and sizes and injuries started to fill the waiting room as Kelsey continued to pace along a far wall. It was cool, the air-conditioning a low hum in the background and she tugged the zipper of her sweatshirt up to her neck and crossed her arms, her cell phone clenched in her fist.

She wanted desperately to call Jessica, but she didn't want to wake her folks or Jessica's kids, not at four in the morning, especially if she didn't have her cell phone close by.

She'd never felt so alone in her entire life.

Then an elderly lady with gray curls and a gentle smile approached her. "Excuse me, miss? Are you Kelsey Hunt?" she asked.

Kelsey's feet stopped and it felt as if her heart did, as well. She opened her mouth to speak, but nothing came out. She could only nod.

"My name is Mary Macintyre. I'm a volunteer here at the hospital." She touched the ID badge attached to the light blue blazer she wore. "You came in with Mr. Fortune and his son?"

"Yes." The word rushed from her lips. "How is he? How's Anthony?"

"If you will come with me, I'll take you up to the floor where the patient is being treated. Mr. Fortune is waiting there."

Kelsey followed the woman to the elevators. "Do you know—?"

"I'm sorry, Miss Hunt. I'm not at liberty to share any information." The doors slid silently closed and she pressed a button for the sixth floor.

Of course she couldn't.

Kelsey acknowledged her words with a quick nod, her eyes glued to the digital readout that ticked off each floor as they passed it by. The upward motion caused the knots in her stomach to multiply with each floor. Moments later, they were walking down a dimly lit hallway and then the grandmotherly-looking volunteer stopped outside a doorway.

"This is the waiting area for this floor," she said.

She'd looked for signs, something to tell her if this was an intensive care unit or a regular inpatient floor, but there was nothing. Where was she? Was Cooper in there?

She pushed open the door, then paused to offer a shaky smile to the woman. "Thank you for...for bringing me here."

"You're welcome, dear."

Kelsey didn't watch the woman leave. She entered the room, disappointment filling her to find it empty. No Cooper. She moved past the couches and chairs scattered around, drawn to the window that looked out over the bright lights of the city, even at this time of the night.

Kelsey rubbed a hand against her tired eyes, preparing for more waiting. The fact that Anthony was out of the emergency room and in a regular patient's room couldn't be good. Were things so bad that he required hospitalization?

If she could just see Cooper, if he would come and tell her everything was going to be all right—

The door opened and she turned.

Cooper.

Relief flooded her veins. Then he moved forward into the soft lighting provided by a few table lamps and the glow of an oversize aquarium. Pain and worry etched every inch of his face.

He stopped and bracketed his hands on his hips, his head falling forward. With his chin tucked close to his chest, defeat and dejection radiated from his entire body.

Did he think she'd left? No, he must've been the one who'd sent for her. She stepped away from the window, the need to be near him, to hold him in her arms washed over her.

"I'm here, Cooper."

His sudden jerky steps backward caused Kelsey to stop before she reached him. She crossed her arms over her chest, then pressed one hand to her mouth for a moment before she forced the question past her dry throat. "How—how is he?"

"They don't know yet." He shoved his hand through his hair, turning away. "It could be an infection or something viral. The doctors are running tests."

An hour at the hospital and they didn't know what was causing a five-month-old to fight to breathe? "Is your cousin with him?"

Cooper nodded, still not looking at her. "Yeah, Jeremy got here right after we did."

"Kirsten, too?"

He glanced at her, confusion on his face for a moment. "No, she's not here. Jeremy said she's fighting a cold herself, so he refused to let her come."

She dropped her hands, her fingers still clenched around her phone. "So, what have the doctors told you?"

"He's got a slight fever and he's dehydrated. Something I should've picked up on considering how few bottles he's finished in the last couple of days, not to mention the dry diapers." He folded his arms across his chest, his words pouring out in an agonizing whisper. "They had to put an IV in…to give him fluids. In his foot. A ventilator might be needed too, if—if he continues to struggle with his breathing."

Cooper's description tore at her heart. Kelsey fought to control the tears that pushed at the outer edges of her eyes. She had to stay calm, to keep it together because she had a feeling the man standing in front of her was inches away from losing control.

"I should've known…" He covered his face with his hands, muffling his words. "I should've known."

"Cooper, you can't blame yourself. When you saw Anthony wasn't feeling well, you called the clinic." Unable to stop herself, Kelsey hurried to his side, laying a hand on his arm. "You did all you could tonight—"

He yanked free from her touch. Pushing past her, his quick strides took him across the room and away from her. "I'm not talking about tonight!"

She turned around, the anguish in his tone held her rooted to the spot. "What then?"

"All of it…everything…" He threw his hands wide and faced her, but his eyes were vacant. "I can't do this! Being responsible, taking care of a child. The right foods, the right toys, the right medicines. Teaching them how to talk, how to eat…how to care, to be responsible, to grow up…"

His jumbled words flew around the room like bullets shot wildly from a gun, shattering the world around her, shattering her heart. "Cooper, you need to calm down—"

"No, what I need to do is what I should've done weeks ago. DNA test be damned! I'm the absolute worst person to be taking care of a child." He slammed a fist to the center of his chest. "Jeremy and Kirsten were amazing with Anthony, Kirsten loves him as if he's her own child. They should be the ones raising him, keeping him safe… keeping him well."

She swallowed back the rise of sobs that filled her throat. "You don't…you don't mean that."

"I never should've stuck around, never should've let myself be distracted by getting involved again with my family, with this town, with you. The doc says this— whatever this sickness is—has probably been building for days. Taking him to the fair was a mistake, going on that picnic was a mistake, being with you was—"

"A mistake?" she cut him off, her words a broken whisper she pushed past her clenched teeth.

"This was wrong, thinking I could have it all." He crossed to the window and stood in the very spot Kelsey had occupied earlier. "I don't belong here. I belong out there. The wide open sky over my head and the hard earth beneath my feet. Horses and cattle…that's what I'm good at, that's all I'm good at. All I'm good for."

Kelsey bit off the urge to scream. It was happening again and she was powerless to stop the pain, sharp and jabbing, that came along with the realization that

Cooper, while still standing in front of her, was already gone.

So she didn't even try. She let it wash over her, the current so strong it left nothing in its wake but the wreckage that once was her heart.

Opening her mouth, she spoke with a calmness that came only from the numbness filling her soul. "If you can't see where you belong, then I feel sorry for you, Cooper Fortune. If you've decided to leave, then you should just go."

Chapter Thirteen

Had he heard her right? Cooper's head snapped around. Kelsey had told him to leave?

"What did you say?"

"You heard me."

She wasn't going to fight him on this. He could see it in her eyes. She wasn't going to beg him to stay like so many others had done.

All his life he'd walked away, starting with his mother, who'd pleaded with him to stick around after he'd graduated high school. She'd had elaborate plans and promises of making life better for him, for their entire family.

He'd walked away from ranch owners who didn't want to lose his hard work ethic and long-earned skills, away from friends who'd claimed they'd miss the shared camaraderie, away from women who told him they'd given him their hearts.

Walking away was what he did.

It was what had always worked for him.

No ties, no binds. No pain.

No gut-wrenching ache like he'd experienced the moment the doctor had taken Anthony from his arms, as if his heart had been ripped out of his chest.

He'd stood helpless in that tiny examining room as medical people swarmed over his son, unable to do anything but listen as Anthony's cries died to faint whimpers because he didn't have the air in his tiny lungs to make any more noise. And he thought about how he'd failed.

He'd failed in his promise to take care of the child he'd created, the child he'd known less than a month. There'd been nothing he could do for Anthony except sign the paperwork that had allowed the medical staff to poke and prod and test, whatever it took to save his son's life.

What a fool he'd been to think that caring for a baby was easy, fun…doable. Especially for a guy like him.

"You don't—" Unable to hold Kelsey's gaze any longer, Cooper looked past her to the waiting room door.

Ten steps, twelve at the most, and he was out of here.

An hour and he'd be gone from Red Rock. A day would have him out of the State of Texas altogether.

"You can't even begin to understand."

"I don't have to. You've made your decision." Kelsey's voice was cool, her words sharp as they cut deep into his skin, digging for bone as she backed toward the door. "And if you're going to do what you've always been good at—"

Her voice cracked, but she lifted her chin and tossed

her long ponytail over one shoulder. "Don't expect me to stand here and watch you make the biggest mistake of your life. I'll contact Jeremy in a few days to check up on Anthony. Goodbye, Cooper."

She spun and vanished out the door.

Cooper closed his eyes, trying to ignore the bright, white flash that exploded so deep in his soul, it disseminated to the farthest corners of his being. He ceased to exist, despite his body still functioning. He accepted that the man he knew, the man he was, no longer mattered.

Kelsey didn't love him.

She'd walked away.

Stumbling to the door, he forced his eyes to open and his feet to carry him to the elevator. As soon as it opened, he fell inside, slammed the button for the ground floor and waited until he was finally able to walk out the glass doors and into the inky blackness of the night.

He was doing the right thing.

For him, for Anthony...for everyone.

Seconds later, he gunned his truck's engine and tore out of the parking lot as if all the demons of hell were on his tail. Looking into the rearview mirror, he watched the hospital, and his life, fade into the distance.

"Kelsey?"

She heard her name being called, a soft whisper that carried through the mechanical beeps and whirls that filled the air. She couldn't turn around, couldn't look away from the little boy resting peacefully on the bed in front of her.

"Kels?"

Warm fingers touched hers. She looked down and found a familiar hand. She turned and fell into her sister's arms. Tears burned as they filled her eyes and spilled over to her cheeks. Jessica held her tightly, rocking back and forth, caressing her back.

She tried to pull herself together, but the warmth and protection of her sister's arms made it so easy to let the devastation bubble forth and pour from her. "He's gone, Jess. Cooper's gone. He couldn't handle the pain, his own or Anthony's. This poor little baby is fighting—something—and his father isn't by his side like he should be."

Her breathing shuddered as she fought to put her jumbled emotions into words. "He said he can't be a father, but he's wrong, he's a great father! I've been waiting…so sure he'd turn around and come back…to his son. To me. He can't just walk away. He can't."

"Shh, it's okay, sweetie." Her sister led her to the small couch at the far side of the room. "Come on, let's sit for a minute."

Surprised that she was still on her feet, Kelsey followed Jessica's lead. Dropping to the soft cushions, she laid her head against her sister's shoulder. "How did you know I was here?"

"Dr. Fortune called me."

Of course he did.

After she'd walked out on Cooper, left him standing alone in the waiting room before he could leave her, she'd found the ladies' room just down the hall. When she'd emerged, she'd run straight into Jeremy.

He'd quickly reassured her that while they were still waiting on test results, Anthony was in stable condition. Jeremy then asked where Cooper was, saying he wasn't in the waiting room, and she'd answered him honestly—she didn't know. His reaction was difficult to read, but he remained silent as he took her to Anthony's room, promising her it was okay to be there.

She didn't know how much time had passed. Her focus had been solely on the little boy as he slept—without a ventilator, thank goodness, but still hooked up with tubing and wires to the equipment and monitors surrounding the child-size bed.

She lifted her gaze and looked out the window. The city skyline was still dark. "What time is it?"

"A little after five. I came as soon as I could." Jessica gave her a quick squeeze. "I would've been here sooner if you'd called me."

Kelsey sniffed. "I know. Everything just happened so fast."

Another sniffle and her sister stuck a box of tissues under her nose. Kelsey grabbed a handful. She pushed herself to her feet and moved away, needing a moment to pull herself together. The last thing she wanted was for her crying to wake Anthony.

She dried her eyes, blew her nose and tossed the tissues in the trash. Pulling in a deep breath, she turned around. With her hands clasped together, fingertips pressed to her chin like she was praying, she looked into her sister's compassionate eyes.

"Did I mention Cooper left?"

Jessica nodded. "Yeah, you did."

Kelsey dropped her hands. "I still can't believe it."

"Are you sure he's gone? I mean really gone?" Her sister moved to sit on the edge of the couch. "Maybe he just needed some time to take all this in, to deal with everything."

"You didn't hear him, Jess." Unable to stand still, Kelsey paced across the room, keeping her voice to a low whisper. "He was panicked and angry and scared. He blames himself for this, he blames me—"

Jessica shot to her feet. "You?"

"Maybe not me directly, but he said being with me, getting involved with me, distracted him."

"That's crazy." Her sister's words were a hushed whisper. "It's not like you've been dragging him out to nightclubs or fancy restaurants in the city. You've been helping him take care of his son."

The memories of the last few weeks rushed through Kelsey. The first time she saw Cooper in her barn, the first time she saw Anthony in his father's arms. Her holding Anthony as he slept, being held in Cooper's arms after making love, the moment—just a few hours ago—when she'd realized she'd fallen in love with both of them.

The tears returned and she dropped her head, her gaze centered on her hands. "I told him to leave."

Jessica walked to stand in front of her. "What?"

"When he said it would be better if he left, I told him if that was his decision, then he needed to go." She lifted her face, brushing away the wetness from her cheeks. "I can't go my whole life wondering when or if Cooper is going to take off. That's not fair to me and certainly not fair to that sweet boy over there. Cooper has a great family and he has—*had* me, but I guess that wasn't enough."

"Oh, sweetie."

"But now I'm wondering if I was wrong to say those things. If he left because—"

"No, don't even think that way," Jess interrupted,

pulling out her best "mama" voice and waving a finger in Kelsey's face. "Cooper Fortune is a man who makes his own decisions, no matter how stupid they might be."

A smile came to Kelsey's lips, but the dull ache shimmering inside of her soon erased it. She turned to look at Anthony. "What am I going to do, Jess? I know this little boy has a wonderful family, but he's become so important to me."

"You'll keep doing exactly what you're doing now. You'll be there for him in any way you can."

Kelsey's heart throbbed as the love she felt for Anthony overflowed, but it couldn't wash away the part of her that still belonged to one special man. "Okay, I can do that. Now what do I do about my broken heart?"

The traffic light changed from green to red.

It skipped over the cautionary yellow and Cooper slammed on the brakes and his truck lurched to a stop.

"What the hell? How is that even possible?" His ragged voice echoed in the silence of his truck. He shook his head and scrubbed a hand across his eyes.

Looking around, he realized he'd taken the wrong turn off the highway, thanks to the stinging tears that ignored his command to stop. He'd landed in a suburb right at the San Antonio city limits.

His was the only vehicle at the four-way intersection. Hell, he was the only one on the entire road of one- and two-story homes with large, toy-strewn yards on either side of the tree-lined street.

A warm breeze sifted through the open window of his truck as he took it all in. He clenched his fingers around the steering wheel, watching as a child-size swing attached to a low branch of a nearby oak tree swayed back and forth.

An image formed in his mind of a family enjoying a sunny day, kids playing in the yard, a mother exiting the home to stand on the covered porch with a tray in her hands while a father pushed a toddler in that swing.

The perfect family, living in a world that he'd believed was only possible in his dreams.

The man turned to him and waved. Cooper lifted his hand to respond as confusion bled into bewilderment... that was his own face reflected back. The father was him.

The child in the swing laughed with delight and the woman walked down the front steps, smiling at the group of children surrounding her, one boy—almost as tall as she was—reached for a drink off the tray, then turned. His sweet face belonged to Anthony...

"Oh, God, what have I done?"

The pain inside his head, inside his heart exploded and the image shattered into a thousand pieces. A wrenching cry tore from his mouth in an agonized breath that seared his lungs, as if it'd been held too long.

The light flashed green and he swung his truck into the closest driveway, checked to make sure the road was still clear and whipped out again, heading back in the direction he'd come. The clock on the radio told him it was almost five.

How long had he been gone? Was it too late?

No, it couldn't be.

He didn't have any idea how he'd found his way back

to the hospital, but he parked and ran for the elevator, his lips moving in a silent prayer.

Don't let me be too late. Please...

He exited back onto the sixth floor and headed for the waiting room. She had to be there. Kelsey had to be—

Shock froze him in the doorway as he took in the number of people filling the space.

His brother, Ross, stood near the window, speaking on his cell phone, his wife, Julie, is his arms. Frannie and Roberto occupied one of the couches while JR and Isabella sat together opposite them, their hands locked together over her emerging stomach, round with their first child. His cousins Nick and Darr Fortune—JR's brothers, stood in a tight huddle of hushed conversation near the fish tank.

"Cooper?" Ross called his name. Everyone turned to look at him. "Is everything okay?"

"Ah, what—what are you all doing here?"

With his cell phone still at his ear, Ross crossed to the room to stand in front of him. "Jeremy called me, I called JR and it just snowballed from there. We're your family, Anthony's family. Where else would we be?"

Cooper didn't know what to say. It had never occurred to him to contact anyone, but here they were, Fortunes standing strong to support him. The notion humbled him beyond belief.

"Jeremy came by about fifteen minutes ago and told us that Anthony's stable," Ross continued. "He had an emergency with one of his patients and had to leave, but he said a great team of doctors is working on finding out what's wrong with the baby. He was also looking for you."

Stable. Anthony was stable.

Relief washed over him, but along with that feeling came more questions. Were the doctors finally able to figure out what had caused his son's erratic breathing? Was Anthony hooked up to even more machines?

"Cooper?"

He jerked his head, realizing he'd missed something and found his brother waving a cell phone in front of his face.

"I know you have to get back to Anthony," Ross said, "but Flint's on the line. He wants to know if you need him to come home?"

Cooper grabbed the phone and put it to his ear. "Hey, bro...ah, everyone—well, not every Fortune, but there's a crowd here so I don't think—" He paused, swallowing hard at his brother's words. "Yeah, I know for a while there you thought he might be yours...okay, uncle, if you can make it...yes, I want you here."

He pressed a button to end the call and handed Ross back his phone. "He's at the Denver airport already. His flight leaves in less than an hour."

Ross grinned. "Sounds like Flint."

Looking around the room, Cooper acknowledged the rest of his family with a nod of his head, but what he was really doing was looking for one special person. "Has anyone seen Kelsey?"

A murmur of negative responses and shaking of heads caused the crack in his heart to splinter completely, one half plummeting to his feet.

She'd left? She'd dashed out of the waiting room after telling him to leave, but he never dreamed she'd actually leave the hospital.

He couldn't believe it. Didn't want to believe it. Of

course, he hadn't bothered to look for her when he ran, but he was back and dammit—he'd actually expected her to be here.

And he had no one to blame for that but himself.

He clenched his teeth until his jaw ached as the memory of what he'd said to her flowed through him. Kelsey was gone, but she couldn't have gone far, even if she'd managed to get a ride back to Red Rock. He said a quick prayer that it wasn't too late—that he hadn't completely damaged any hope for the future, but right now his son's health had to be his number-one priority.

He took a step backward. "I need to go."

Ross nodded. "Of course, get back to your son. Just let us know once they've given him the all-clear."

"You all don't have to stay—"

"We'll be here." Ross, JR, Nick and Darr all spoke the same words, their voices a collective show of family unity.

Cooper could only nod in response and headed down the hall. Stopping first to identify himself to the staff at the nursing station, he took a few minutes to wash his hands before hurrying to Anthony's room. He paused to pull in a fortifying breath and reached for the door.

"Where do you think you're going?" A feminine hand pressed against his chest, stopping him in his tracks.

Cooper looked down, shocked to see a pair of familiar brown eyes staring back at him. "To see my son."

Those eyes narrowed in anger. "And my sister."

A loud buzzing exploded in his head, a sound he hadn't heard since his rodeo days at the end of a kickass, eight-second ride. The intensity of it nearly stole his ability to speak. "Kels...Kelsey's here?"

"Where else would she be?" Jessica stepped closer

until there was barely an inch of air between them. "She loves that little boy, almost as much as she lov—"

She cut off her own words. Cooper bit down hard on his inner cheek to stop himself from demanding she finish her sentence. The buzzing in his head morphed into a whisper, a promise for a different life. A better life than the one he'd been living until the moment he'd found out about his son.

Until he'd met Kelsey.

"What? No comeback?" Their eyes locked and Jessica dropped her hand. "You know, not everyone gets the opportunity to right a wrong they've done. The fact that you're here when my sister thinks you're halfway to Wyoming...I hope that means you finally get it."

He did.

Kelsey's sister didn't have to explain what "it" was. He knew. Nothing was more important to Cooper than the two people on the other side of this door. He'd prayed the whole way back to the hospital that he wasn't too late to convince Kelsey of that. It had never occurred to him he might have to convince her family, too, but if that's what it took, that's what he'd do.

"I want a second chance," he said, looking into Jessica's eyes somehow knowing Kelsey had told her everything that had happened between them tonight. "I *need* a second chance."

She moved out of his way. "If you screw this up, if you ever make my sister cry again—"

"I won't. I promise."

He stepped inside and found the room dark except for the soft light directing his gaze to his son who was smiling and awake in the bed. Four quick strides had him by Anthony's side, reaching for the tiny fist the baby waved at him.

"Hey there, little guy." His heart lurched when Anthony's fingers wrapped around his index finger and held on tight.

Looking over his son from his head to his feet, he noted the ease with which his chest rose and fell, even with the electrodes that hooked him up to a heart monitor and the IV that provided a steady drip of fluids.

Cooper leaned over the bed, one hand caressing Anthony's baby-fine hair. He curled his fingers around the baby's hand, drawing it up gently to his lips for a kiss. He lowered his head and found his son looking at him with a solemn expression on his face. The love and trust he saw in those brown eyes caused Cooper to lock his shaky knees. He opened his mouth, but nothing came out. Snapping it closed again, he swallowed hard and then let the first thought in his head fall from his lips.

"Please forgive me," he rasped, "for walking away. I never should've left you…I never will again. You can count on that. I'm going to be here to love and take care of you. Forever."

Anthony responded by smiling and trying to roll toward him.

"Hey there, none of that." Cooper pressed gently to the baby's shoulder. "You need to lie still, little guy."

"Easier said than done." The soft words came from the far side of Anthony's bed. "But that's true for most things, I guess."

Cooper jerked upright at the sound of her voice.

Kelsey.

She stood less than two feet away, but with her arms folded tightly over her chest and the pain of what he'd done reflected in her eyes, she was further away from him than when they first met.

"He's been pretty lively for the last ten minutes or so since the nurse was in here putting in a new bag of fluid for the IV," she continued, putting her focus on Anthony.

The baby reacted to her voice, turning his head to look at her. She reached out to still his movements, but at the last moment, curled her fingers into a fist and pulled back.

"Kels…"

"The nurse wouldn't tell me anything, of course, but she did say that the doctors would be here in a few moments to talk to you." She looked at him again. "Looks like you got back just in time."

Cooper headed around the end of the bed. "Kels, please—"

She sidestepped him, grabbing her purse from a nearby chair and heading for the door. "Well, I'll be leaving since I'm not needed here anymore."

His hands itched to reach for her, to touch her, to stop her. Is that how she'd felt when he walked out? He had to do something, say something, to keep her here. "You're wrong. I need you."

Chapter Fourteen

Cooper's soft words tore at Kelsey's heart. Deep down she knew they weren't true. "Don't worry about me having a ride. My sister's here—"

"I know. I just talked to her."

Kelsey stopped and turned to him. "You did? Where?"

"Out in the hall."

She closed her eyes for a long moment, before opening them to look directly at him. "What did she say to you?"

"Not much." He walked slowly toward her.

She knew she should back away, not let him get any closer, but the intensity in his dark eyes held her rooted to the spot.

"But she did make it pretty clear that if I ever hurt you again like I did today, she'd skin me alive, cut my hide into tiny pieces and make sure no one could find the leftovers."

"She did not!" Kelsey gasped.

"Damn straight I did," came the muffled reply through the crack in the door.

Kelsey spun around and yanked open the heavy wooden door. Her sister stumbled into the room, then righted herself quickly, a blameless gleam in her eyes.

"Jessica! Are you crazy?"

Her sister jabbed a finger in Cooper's direction. "No crazier than this cowboy who can't seem to figure out which direction he's heading."

"I know exactly where I'm heading...now."

Cooper's hands settled on Kelsey's shoulders. She jumped at his heated touch, not realizing he'd moved in behind her.

He gave her a gentle squeeze, then loosened his grip, but kept his hands firmly in place. "And if you'd give me a chance, Kelsey, I'll keep that promise."

His words had Kelsey looking back at him over her shoulder. "What promise?"

Jessica slipped back out of the room and Kelsey allowed Cooper to turn her to face him. He slowly trailed his hands down her arms from her shoulders to her wrists. His gentle stroke took her back to Sunday night at his cottage when he'd touched her the same way, right before he gave her the option of walking away. Was he going to do the same thing now?

Was he trying to let her down easy? Was that his promise?

Like that was even possible.

She couldn't deal with it again. Especially while his impassioned speech to Anthony for forgiveness still rang in her ears. He loved his son, and she was grateful he'd realized that and returned to the hospital, but that had nothing to do with her.

Cooper started to lace her fingers with his; the tingling sensation of his touch was too much to bear. She scooted away, not getting very far, however, when her backside bumped against the closed door.

"Kelsey—"

She held up her hand, as if to physically stop him from speaking. "I don't know what you said to my sister—"

"I told her what I'm trying to tell you," Cooper spoke over her, a hint of exasperation in his tone. "I was wrong, Kelsey. Wrong about everything that happened back in that waiting room. I never should've walked out on Anthony...on you."

He paused, as if he expected her to reply. Her shock at his words had her opening her mouth, but her inability to speak had her snapping it closed again.

"I said some stupid things to you, terrible things," he continued, softer and filled with regret. "I panicked and almost threw away the best thing that has ever happened to me."

Almost?

Joy gushed to life deep inside her, but she quickly snuffed it out. "You don't mean that."

"Yes, I do. Thanks to the asinine way I acted, you have every right to think that—to say that—" He took a step toward her, then stopped, his hands dropping to his sides. "And this all must sound crazy compared to how I ranted at you before, but I had a...a moment...I can't really explain it. I know now that finding out about Anthony, finding you, saved me from a life that was all wrong, a life I never even realized I didn't want—until you and Anthony showed me what was possible, with a little healing and a lot of love."

She slowly shook her head, trying to ignore the stricken look that crossed his face. "I can't heal you like you're one of my rescue horses, Cooper. If you are going to be 'saved,' you need to save yourself."

"I know. And it's up to me to make things different, better, for myself. I'm also smart enough to know I'm a work in progress." He offered a halfhearted shrug. "Hell, a man can't change a way of thinking, knee-jerk reactions, or brainless decision-making that easily, especially after living a certain way his entire life. I'll screw up again somewhere down the line, but that's not going to stop me from doing my damnedest to be a better man. The kind of man who deserves a woman like you."

"Cooper, I—"

"I love you, Kelsey Hunt." He slowly walked toward her. "I've never said that to a woman before. In fact, the only other person I've ever said that to is lying right over there."

He looked at the hospital bed where Anthony had fallen back into a peaceful sleep. Kelsey saw steadfastness in his gaze, mixed with an easy contentment, and she couldn't stop herself from taking his hand.

He turned to look at her again, his eyes bright with unshed tears. "I love my son and I love you. My plan is to repeat those words to both of you. Often. Please believe me, Kelsey. I love you so much."

"I—I don't know what to say."

"Say I'm not too late." He cupped her cheek and she couldn't stop herself from leaning into his touch.

"Tell me you forgive me," he whispered against her temple. "Tell me that you love me, too."

She melted into him. "I do love you."

Her breathy rush of words caused his hand to tighten involuntarily in her hair. "Really?"

Kelsey smiled and moved into his arms, loving how they encircled her with warmth and strength. "Yes, really."

His lips moved softly over hers in a kiss that held the promise of his love and a shared future. "Thank you, thank you."

A knock at the door had Kelsey stepping back out of his arms, but Cooper held her close to his side as the young doctor who'd met them at the ER entrance hours ago walked into the room.

"Well, we have news about your son," Dr. Stanhope said as he flipped open the chart in his hands. "Due to the symptoms Anthony exhibited when he arrived, and a blood test that showed him with a higher white blood cell count than normal, we initially thought he was suffering from respiratory syncytial virus, also known as RSV. For most children, RSV isn't much different from a standard cold with a cough, runny nose and a low-grade fever. However, some kids also suffer from an inflammation of the lung's air tubes, which, in a child of Anthony's age, are very small. That's what happened in your son's case."

Kelsey bit on her lower lip, trying to hold back her tears at the doctor's diagnosis. Cooper stiffened, his arm tightening around her waist.

"So he has bronchitis?" he asked.

"Actually, it's called bronchiolitis in infants and despite your son's mild symptoms, the onset was fast. You'll want to make sure his primary care doctor keeps an eye on his lung development once this infection has cleared up. We're replenishing his fluids with the IV, and he's still a bit raspy, but the good news is, he's responding to treatment, and we expect a full recovery."

"He's really going to be okay?" Kelsey asked.

"Yes, he really is. We're going to keep him for the day, just to make sure." The doctor smiled as he closed the file, his focus on Cooper. "Then, Mrs. Fortune, you'll be free to take your family home."

Kelsey's face heated at the doctor's assumption. "Oh, I'm not—"

"Going anywhere, yes, dear, we know." Cooper cut off her words with a quick kiss to her forehead. He then released her in order to hold out his hand. "We're staying until Anthony is released. Thank you, Doctor. We appreciate all you've done."

The doctor shook Cooper's hand and Kelsey's when she offered it as well. "You're both welcome, and don't worry about bringing the little one to the hospital. My wife and I are new parents, too, and it can be a bit scary sometimes."

"And wonderful," Kelsey said, happiness filling her. She now understood the meaning of Cooper's assurance that they were both here for Anthony. "It's wonderful, as well."

"I thought you said you had it."

Cooper spoke in a hushed whisper as he and Flint stood in the hallway off the kitchen of the main house at the Double Crown Ranch. Everyone—and he did mean everyone—had come to the ranch today at Lily's request for a party to officially welcome Anthony to the Fortune family.

The last time there'd been this many Fortunes and

Mendozas together in one place had been at what was supposed to have been Lily and William's wedding, back on New Year's Eve.

He wondered if Lily thought of that as she moved around the expansive back patio, making sure everyone had enough to eat and drink. She kept returning to check on William, too, who'd chosen to sit on the outskirts of the party at an umbrella-covered table.

"Didn't I give it to you already?" Flint patted his hands over his pockets, first his shirt, then his jeans, a wide grin on his face.

"Don't play games with me, little brother. Not today."

"Geez, you become a father and fall in love and suddenly you're no fun anymore." Flint yanked out a small velvet box from his back pocket and tossed it to his brother. "It's a beauty. When did you find the time to shop?"

"I spotted it when I took Anthony to the clinic on Saturday for a follow-up visit." Cooper popped open the lid and looked down at the square-cut diamond flanked by two blue topazes, Anthony and Kelsey's birthstones, as both were born in December. "It's perfect. Thanks for picking it up."

"You plan on doing this here? Today?"

Cooper smiled. "Yep."

"You sure Kelsey is going to give you the right answer? The answer you want?"

He was a hundred percent sure and even spoke with Kelsey's father a few minutes ago about his intentions.

He'd found Jack Hunt to be a soft-spoken man with a humorous gleam in his eye, but he was also serious when it came to his family. Jack had asked some pointed questions that Cooper answered honestly, then he shook Cooper's hand and welcomed him to the family. "Yeah, I'm sure."

Flint just shook his head and walked toward the outside patio where the party was taking place.

Cooper fell into step behind him, but ended up walking right into him when Flint stopped suddenly. "Whoa, what'd you run into?"

Flint pointed at his leg. "This."

Cooper looked down and grinned when he saw the little kid who'd latched himself tightly to Flint's pant leg.

The boy looked up at the two brothers. "Hi."

"Hi, yourself," Flint replied, then glanced at Cooper. "Who does this rug rat belong to?"

"Hard to say." Cooper grinned. "I think the majority of the people here today are under four feet tall."

"Adam, there you are!"

Jessica hurried across the family room toward them. She reached for the boy who in turn only clung tighter to Flint's pants.

Dropping to her knees, she worked to peel the tiny fingers from the starched khaki material. "Adam, you're supposed to be with your sister. Now, let go of this gentleman."

"No!"

"I'm really sorry about this." She looked upward, a heated blush on her cheeks that deepened when her gaze landed on Flint's face. She then looked at Cooper and her eyes grew wide. "Cooper."

"Hey, Jess."

Flint bracketed his hands on his hips. "I take it you two know each other?"

"Jess, this is my brother, Flint Fortune." Cooper gestured with a wave of his hand. "Flint, this is Jessica Hunt-Myers… Kelsey's sister."

It took a moment, but Cooper saw his brother make the connection. Having driven directly to the hospital when his plane had landed in San Antonio last Wednesday, Flint had walked into Anthony's hospital room with a furry teddy bear under one arm, and found Kelsey napping on the couch, her head on Cooper's lap. Cooper managed not to wake her as he slid free, knowing the surprised look on his brother's face would be followed by questions. A lot of questions. They'd gone for coffee and Cooper filled him in on everything—from Anthony's diagnosis to falling in love with Kelsey—including his early-morning run-in with her sister.

"It's nice to meet you, Flint," Jessica huffed as she worked on her son's hands. Finally freeing them from Flint's pants, she stood with the boy in her arms. "And this is my son, Adam."

Flint grinned at the kid. "Hey, Adam."

The little boy smiled in return and then turned to his mother. "I like him, Mama. I choose him."

Cooper didn't have any idea what the little boy was talking about, but the blush on Jessica's face deepened.

"Sweetie, I told you it doesn't work that way." She addressed her son in a low whisper. "Mr. Fortune isn't a piece of candy."

Cooper barked out a laugh, but choked it off when his brother shot him a dark look.

"Excuse me?" Flint asked.

"No, I didn't mean—it's just that Adam is on this kick about picking out a—um, well…"

"Candy?"

"No," Adam spouted with a wide grin, "I want a new da—"

Jessica clapped her fingers over her son's mouth, cutting off his words. "I really should get back to the rest of my brood. Cooper, I think Kelsey was looking for you. Flint, it was nice to meet you."

Jessica hurried away, weaving her way around the leather couch and coffee table, Adam waving at the two of them over her shoulder. Cooper waved back, then noticed his brother's gaze glued to his future sister-in-law's swaying hips.

"Flint?" He waited until his brother turned to look at him, not buying the innocent, boyish look he'd seen many times over the years. "No."

"What?"

"Don't even think about it. She's a mother."

"I sort of figured that out, Coop."

"You're a player and she's not even in the game." He took a step closer, keeping his voice low. "She's a widow with four kids, all under the age of eight."

Flint's eyebrows rose. "Four?"

Cooper held up four fingers as he followed Jessica's path outside.

He spotted Kelsey across the patio, talking with Jeremy, Kirsten and her brother, Max. Kirsten was holding Anthony in her arms and Cooper was glad to see that both of them had recovered from their colds in time for the party.

It still caused his heart to miss a beat every time he thought about that horrible night in the hospital with his son.

He headed for Kelsey, but stopped to shake hands

with Marcos Mendoza and Wendy Fortune, who had catered the party today, and to give Lily a quick kiss of thanks for opening her home to everyone.

"You are an amazing lady," he said after he returned her hug. "Has anyone ever told you that?"

Her gaze flicked off to one side, and Cooper realized she was looking at William before she turned to him again with a serene smile on her face. "Yes, a few someones, a time or two."

"Is all of this too much for him?"

Lily shook her head, knowing exactly who he was asking about. "William's quiet and a bit withdrawn, but he's also relaxed and just…observing. If that's all he can give today, that's enough. Now, let me go check on the children."

Cooper wasn't sure which generation of children she was referring to, William's sons or the young ones running around. He continued toward Kelsey, walking up behind her and wrapping his arms around her waist.

"Hey, you," he whispered in her ear before brushing her long hair off one bare shoulder to drop a quick kiss there. He loved the red dress she wore that left her shoulders, arms and legs bare.

"Where have you been?" Kelsey whispered back, turning her head to look at him as she leaned onto his chest. "You took off after your brother as soon as Flint arrived."

"Oh, just guy talk." He gave her another kiss, then nodded a hello to his cousin. "You keeping an eye on my kid, doc?"

"He's doing just fine," Jeremy said with a smile. "Hard to believe after the way he looked five days ago."

"Thank goodness," Kirsten added as she gave Anthony a quick squeeze. "I don't know what I would've done if something— Well, if something had happened..."

Cooper nodded, knowing exactly what she was saying as Kelsey moved to stand at his side. "We all feel the same."

"You're a good father," Max added. "I'm glad Anthony found his way home to you."

It meant a lot to Cooper that these three people felt that way, as they'd been the first ones to take Anthony into their home, and their hearts, and care for him. "Thank you for saying that, and thank you for all you did for Anthony."

Anthony held out his arms and Cooper took him, holding him close to his chest. When his son reached out and laid a tiny palm against his cheek, he knew he wasn't going to repeat the mistakes his own parents had made. He had the opportunity right now to have the life he'd so envied when he was growing up—a stable, loving one, surrounded by family.

A family that included everyone here this afternoon. Most important, a family that included Kelsey and Anthony.

And now was the perfect time to make that happen.

"Hey, could I have everyone's attention, please?" Cooper called out as he walked backward to the center of the patio, pulling a bewildered Kelsey along with him.

"What are you doing?" she asked, tugging on his hand.

He just smiled and shook his head as everyone quieted

down. The Fortunes, Mendozas and Hunts gathered in a wide circle on the patio and the grassy area beyond.

"First, I'd like to thank all of you for coming this afternoon," Cooper said, facing the crowd, "and I'd especially like to thank Lily for having this crazy, noisy mob in her home."

Cheers erupted and glasses were raised in salute for several minutes, before everyone grew silent again.

"I'm not one for making big speeches," he continued, "but I've come to recognize over the last few weeks, and especially the last few days, that life is such a blessing, and that my long, rocky path has led me to this wonderful child and a bright future."

He looked over at his brothers and sister, standing close by with their families. "It feels good to be home again, with my family, with all of you, but it wasn't until I met this very special lady here…"

He turned to face Kelsey, loving the brilliant joy shining from her eyes as she gazed at him. "It wasn't until I met Kelsey that I realized something very important was missing."

Letting go of her hand, he pulled out the small jewelry box from his pocket and opened it. A collective gasp from the crowd turned into more cheers, applause and whistles as he took out the ring and dropped to one knee in front of her. Balancing Anthony's weight with his own, he looked up and found Kelsey, eyes filled with tears, staring at him.

"I love you with all my heart, Kels, and I'd be honored—we, Anthony and I—would be honored if you agreed to share your life with us."

He held out the ring to her. "Marry me, Kelsey."

She quickly nodded her head. "Yes."

The cheering increased as Cooper rose and slid the diamond onto her finger. He wrapped his arm around her, pulling her close, and their lips met in a light, teasing kiss that held the promise of a wonderful future.

"I love you, Cooper Fortune," she whispered.

"I love you, too."

Moments later they were inundated with hugs and well-wishes from everyone around them. They accepted congratulations and the party continued as the families celebrated together.

Cooper felt a tug on his arm and he turned to find his fiancée had returned to his side.

"Do you realize my sister is taking all the credit for us ending up together?" Kelsey asked with a smile.

He grinned and gave her a quick wink. "That's fine with me. Did she tell you that little Adam has taken quite a liking to my brother, Flint?"

"No, she didn't. I'll have to talk to her about that in a minute, but first I've noticed your uncle William looking over here at you and Anthony," she continued as she took his hand. "Why don't we go over and see him? I don't think he's been introduced to your son yet."

"Our son."

She smiled. "Our son."

"I think that's a great idea," Cooper said.

Tears of joy threatened to spill over from Lily's eyes as Kelsey and Cooper headed their way. They joined her and William where they sat with JR, Isabella, Ross and Julie at one of the outdoor dining tables.

She was so happy for the couple, and even happier that Cooper felt comfortable enough with his family to share such a special moment with all of them.

There would be another Fortune wedding soon, and

despite the sharp pang to her heart with the knowledge it wouldn't be her own, it truly was a wonderful thing.

She brushed away any evidence of her emotions and smiled. "Congratulations, you two."

"Thanks, Lily," Cooper said.

Kelsey sat in the empty chair next to her and took Lily's outstretched hand. She gave it a gentle squeeze before letting go.

Cooper stood in front of William and shifted Anthony from one arm to the other. "Hey, Uncle William, I'm sorry for not getting over here sooner to say hello and for not introducing you to this little guy."

William remained silent, but stared at Anthony with an intense gaze. Lily glanced around, noticing the others were picking up on William's reaction to the baby, as well.

"Anthony, this is my uncle William."

William started to raise his hands, then he dropped them back to his lap. What did that mean? Did he want to…?

"Would you like to hold him?"

William nodded, so Cooper knelt and placed the baby in his uncle's lap, staying close in case he needed to reach for Anthony.

A crowd formed around them as William's other sons, Nick and Darr and their wives, moved closer to the table, watching their father intently.

Holding the infant gently in his arms, William bent his head until it rested against Anthony, who sat contentedly. He stroked the baby's forehead and soon his eyes filled with tears and he began to cry.

Lily's heart lurched in her chest. She wasn't able to hold back a gasp as she clenched her hands close to her heart. Seeing this first true emotional display from the man who'd always shared his sentiments with his family was an incredible moment.

Yes, this is as it should be.

Lily heard the words in her ear as clearly as if someone had whispered them to her. A gentle breeze touched her face and she knew Ryan was letting her know that everything was going to be all right.

This was the sign they'd been waiting for, the sign that the William Fortune they all knew and loved was still in there somewhere.

* * * * *

Look for FORTUNE FOUND,
the next book in
THE FORTUNES OF TEXAS:
LOST...AND FOUND
coming next month to Special Edition.

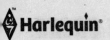
Harlequin®

COMING NEXT MONTH

Available May 31, 2011

#2119 FORTUNE FOUND
Victoria Pade
The Fortunes of Texas: Lost...and Found

#2120 HUSBAND UNDER CONSTRUCTION
Karen Templeton
Wed in the West

#2121 DADDY'S DOUBLE DUTY
Stella Bagwell
Men of the West

#2122 WHAT THE SINGLE DAD WANTS...
Marie Ferrarella
Matchmaking Mamas

#2123 A HOME FOR THE M.D.
Gina Wilkins
Doctors in the Family

#2124 THE TEXAS TYCOON'S BABY
Crystal Green
Billionaire Cowboys, Inc.

SPECIAL EDITION

REQUEST YOUR FREE BOOKS!

2 FREE NOVELS PLUS 2 FREE GIFTS!

◈ Harlequin®

SPECIAL EDITION

Life, Love & Family

YES! Please send me 2 FREE Harlequin Special Edition® novels and my 2 FREE gifts (gifts are worth about $10). After receiving them, if I don't wish to receive any more books, I can return the shipping statement marked "cancel." If I don't cancel, I will receive 6 brand-new novels every month and be billed just $4.24 per book in the U.S. or $4.99 per book in Canada. That's a saving of at least 15% off the cover price! It's quite a bargain! Shipping and handling is just 50¢ per book in the U.S. and 75¢ per book in Canada.* I understand that accepting the 2 free books and gifts places me under no obligation to buy anything. I can always return a shipment and cancel at any time. Even if I never buy another book, the two free books and gifts are mine to keep forever.

235/335 SDN FC7H

Name _____ (PLEASE PRINT)

Address _____ Apt. #

City _____ State/Prov. _____ Zip/Postal Code

Signature (if under 18, a parent or guardian must sign)

Mail to the **Reader Service**:
IN U.S.A.: P.O. Box 1867, Buffalo, NY 14240-1867
IN CANADA: P.O. Box 609, Fort Erie, Ontario L2A 5X3

Not valid for current subscribers to Harlequin Special Edition books.

Want to try two free books from another line?
Call 1-800-873-8635 or visit www.ReaderService.com.

* Terms and prices subject to change without notice. Prices do not include applicable taxes. Sales tax applicable in N.Y. Canadian residents will be charged applicable taxes. Offer not valid in Quebec. This offer is limited to one order per household. All orders subject to credit approval. Credit or debit balances in a customer's account(s) may be offset by any other outstanding balance owed by or to the customer. Please allow 4 to 6 weeks for delivery. Offer available while quantities last.

Your Privacy—The Reader Service is committed to protecting your privacy. Our Privacy Policy is available online at www.ReaderService.com or upon request from the Reader Service.

We make a portion of our mailing list available to reputable third parties that offer products we believe may interest you. If you prefer that we not exchange your name with third parties, or if you wish to clarify or modify your communication preferences, please visit us at www.ReaderService.com/consumerschoice or write to us at Reader Service Preference Service, P.O. Box 9062, Buffalo, NY 14269. Include your complete name and address.

HSE11

Harlequin® Blaze™ brings you
New York Times *and* USA TODAY *bestselling author*
Vicki Lewis Thompson with three new steamy titles
from the bestselling miniseries SONS OF CHANCE

Chance isn't just the last name of these rugged
Wyoming cowboys—it's their motto, too!

Read on for a sneak peek at the first title,
SHOULD'VE BEEN A COWBOY

Available June 2011 only from Harlequin® Blaze™.

"THANKS FOR NOT TURNING ON THE LIGHTS," Tyler said. "I'm a mess."

"Not in my book." Even in low light, Alex had a good view of her yellow shirt plastered to her body. It was all he could do not to reach for her, mud and all. But the next move needed to be hers, not his.

She slicked her wet hair back and squeezed some water out of the ends as she glanced upward. "I like the sound of the rain on a tin roof."

"Me, too."

She met his gaze briefly and looked away. "Where's the sink?"

"At the far end, beyond the last stall."

Tyler's running shoes squished as she walked down the aisle between the rows of stalls. She glanced sideways at Alex. "So how much of a cowboy are you these days? Do you ride the range and stuff?"

"I ride." He liked being able to say that. "Why?"

"Just wondered. Last summer, you were still a city boy. You even told me you weren't the cowboy type, but you're…different now."

He wasn't sure if that was a good thing or a bad thing. Maybe she preferred city boys to cowboys. "How am I different?"

"Well, you dress differently, and your hair's a little longer. Your face seems a little more chiseled, but maybe that's because of your hair. Also, there's something else, something harder to define, an attitude…"

"Are you saying I have an attitude?"

"Not in a bad way. It's more like a quiet confidence."

He was flattered, but still he had to laugh. "I just admitted a while ago that I have all kinds of doubts about this event tomorrow. That doesn't seem like quiet confidence to me."

"This isn't about your job, it's about…your…" She took a deep breath. "It's about your sex appeal, okay? I have no business talking about it, because it will only make me want to do things I shouldn't do." She started toward the end of the barn. "Now, where's that sink? We need to get cleaned up and go back to the house. Dinner is probably ready, and I—"

He spun her around and pulled her into his arms, mud and all. "Let's do those things." Then he kissed her, knowing that she would kiss him back, knowing that this time he would take that kiss where he wanted it to go. And she would let him.

Follow Tyler and Alex's wild adventures in
SHOULD'VE BEEN A COWBOY
Available June 2011 only from Harlequin® Blaze™
wherever books are sold.

HBEXP0611

SPECIAL EDITION

Life, Love and Family

LOVE CAN BE FOUND IN THE MOST UNLIKELY PLACES, ESPECIALLY WHEN YOU'RE NOT LOOKING FOR IT...

Failed marriages, broken families and disappointment. Cecilia and Brandon have both been unlucky in love and life and are ripe for an intervention. Good thing Brandon's mother happens to stumble upon this matchmaking project. But will Brandon be able to open his eyes and get away from his busy career to see that all he needs is right there in front of him?

FIND OUT IN

WHAT THE SINGLE DAD WANTS...

BY *USA TODAY* BESTSELLING AUTHOR

MARIE FERRARELLA

AVAILABLE IN JUNE 2011
WHEREVER BOOKS ARE SOLD.

www.eHarlequin.com

SE0611MF